*When under gelid moon, skies sombre and sable,*
*If your gaze it does turn, up toward starry gables,*
*Behold then the face, in moonlight and beams,*
*Suspended in marble,*
*Our keeper of dreams.*
*For Amy, who keeps me dreaming.*
*A. A.*

*To my parents, for your love and support.*
*To my brothers, for letting me steal these books off your shelves.*
*To Clíodhna, my heart and spine: your light would incinerate Dracula.*
*S. F.*

BIG PICTURE PRESS

First published in the UK in 2024 by Big Picture Press,
an imprint of Bonnier Books UK
5th Floor, HYLO, 103–105 Bunhill Row,
London, EC1Y 8LZ
Owned by Bonnier Books
Sveavägen 56, Stockholm, Sweden
www.bonnierbooks.co.uk

Text copyright © 2024 by Sam Fern
Illustration copyright © 2024 by Adam Allori
Design copyright © 2024 by Big Picture Press

3 5 7 9 10 8 6 4 2

All rights reserved

ISBN 978-1-8007-8342-3

This book was typeset in Gill Sans, Ceria, Caslon Pro,
Helsing, Hoefler text ornaments and Mishelia
The illustrations were created digitally

Edited by Matt Ralphs and Isobel Boston
Designed by Winsome D'Abreu
Production by Neil Randles

Printed in China

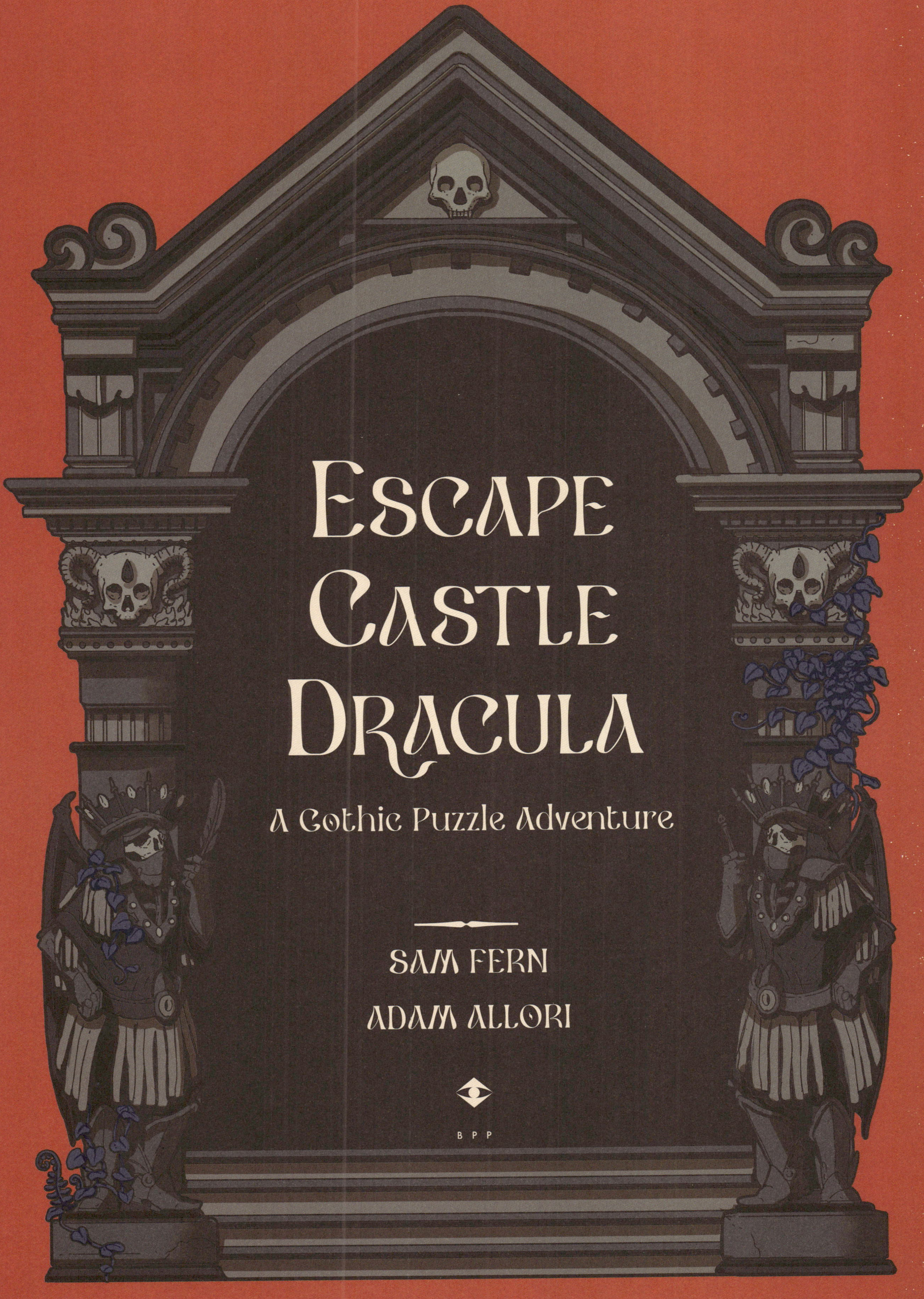

# Escape Castle Dracula

## A Gothic Puzzle Adventure

Sam Fern

Adam Allori

BPP

Dear Guest of Dracula,

I leave this note hidden in your bedchamber to reveal that the Count is not the man you think, or any kind of man at all. Warrior, ruler, scholar, yes – but beneath it all: a vampire!

My name is Abraham van Helsing, professor of supernatural arts. The Count employed me to cast a magical border around Castle Dracula, enabling him to control who may enter or leave. Fool that I am, I did as he asked.

You are his prisoner. Pray he still needs you. As soon as I had finished my work, he set on me in his fanged form and nearly drank me dry!

In return for my life, I offered him my spell-book. Inside it, I have imprisoned twelve monsters: an army fit for a devil! However, I have enchanted the spell-book to give future victims of the Count (such as you) a secret path to freedom, and will hide it before I escape.

Find my spell-book. Open the cover and it will drag you inside. Each page contains a different nightmare, and you must face each villain's trial before the book will let you pass onwards.

Vanquish the final villain, and you will escape Castle Dracula.

Luck and haste,

## Abraham van Helsing

P.S. Should you survive,
find me in Amsterdam.
We must compare notes!

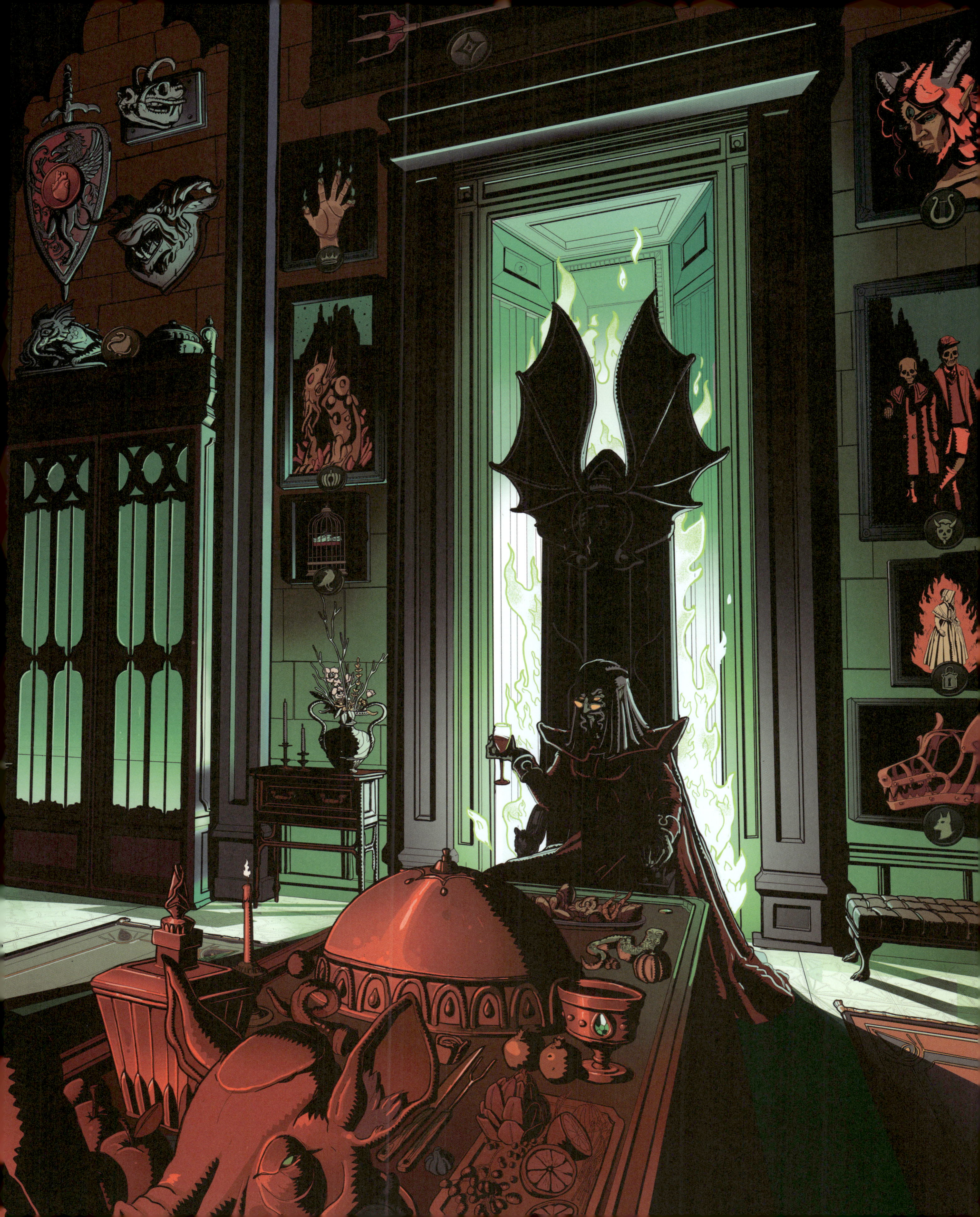

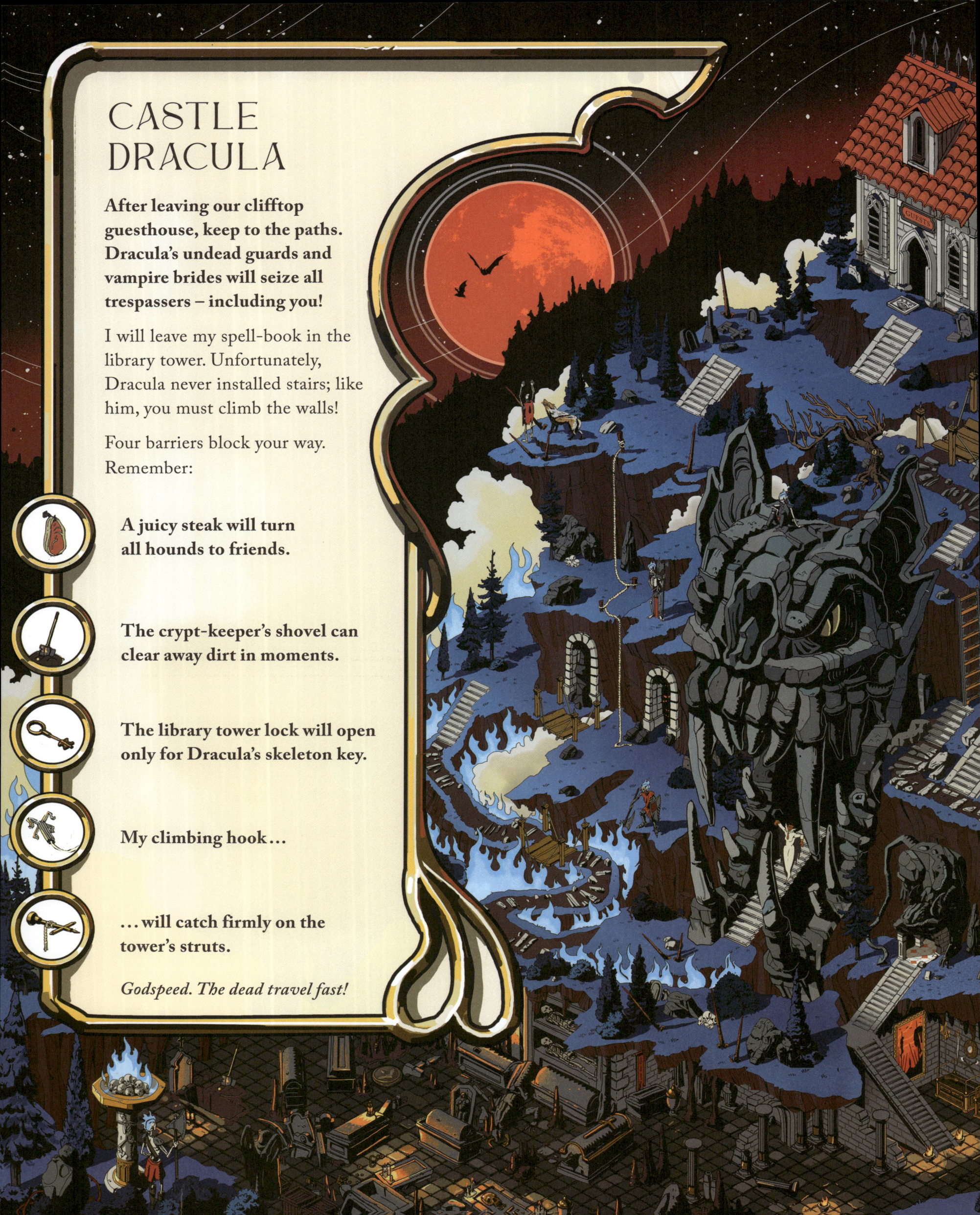

# CASTLE DRACULA

After leaving our clifftop guesthouse, keep to the paths. Dracula's undead guards and vampire brides will seize all trespassers – including you!

I will leave my spell-book in the library tower. Unfortunately, Dracula never installed stairs; like him, you must climb the walls!

Four barriers block your way. Remember:

- A juicy steak will turn all hounds to friends.

- The crypt-keeper's shovel can clear away dirt in moments.

- The library tower lock will open only for Dracula's skeleton key.

- My climbing hook…

- …will catch firmly on the tower's struts.

*Godspeed. The dead travel fast!*

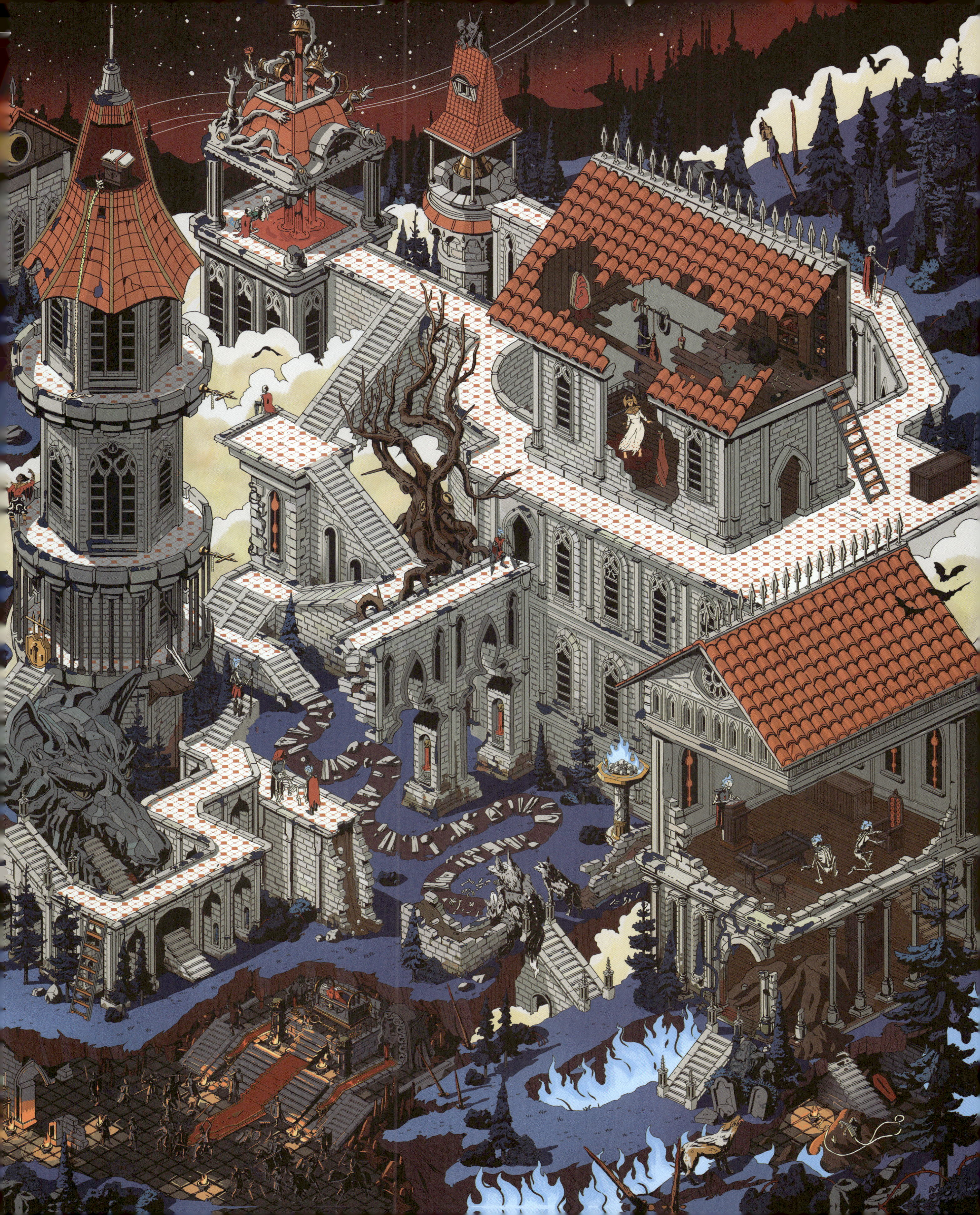

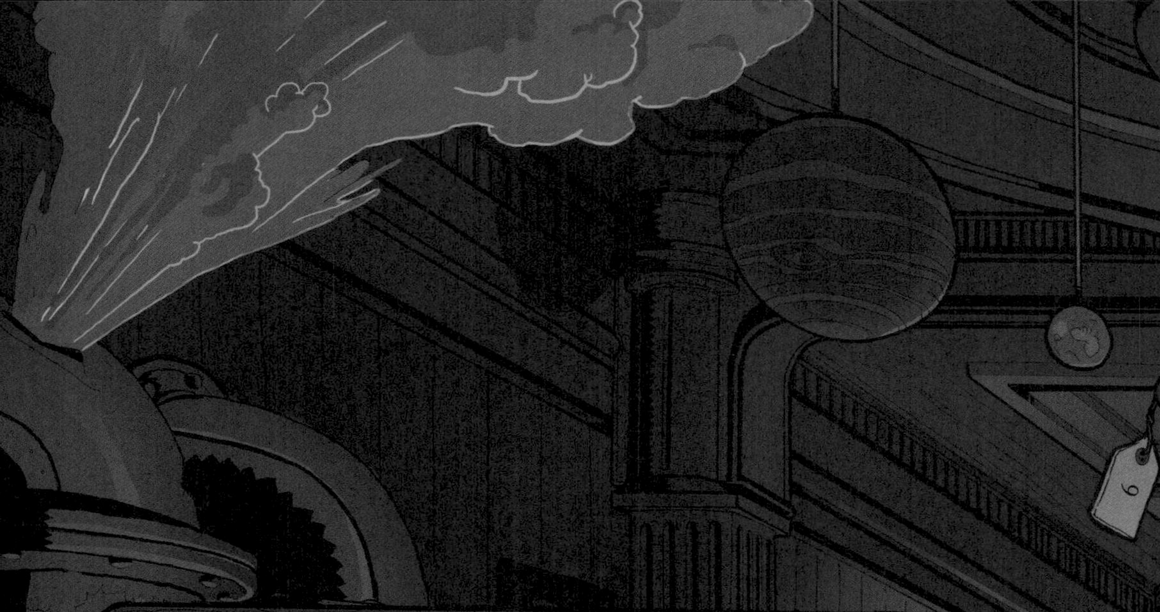

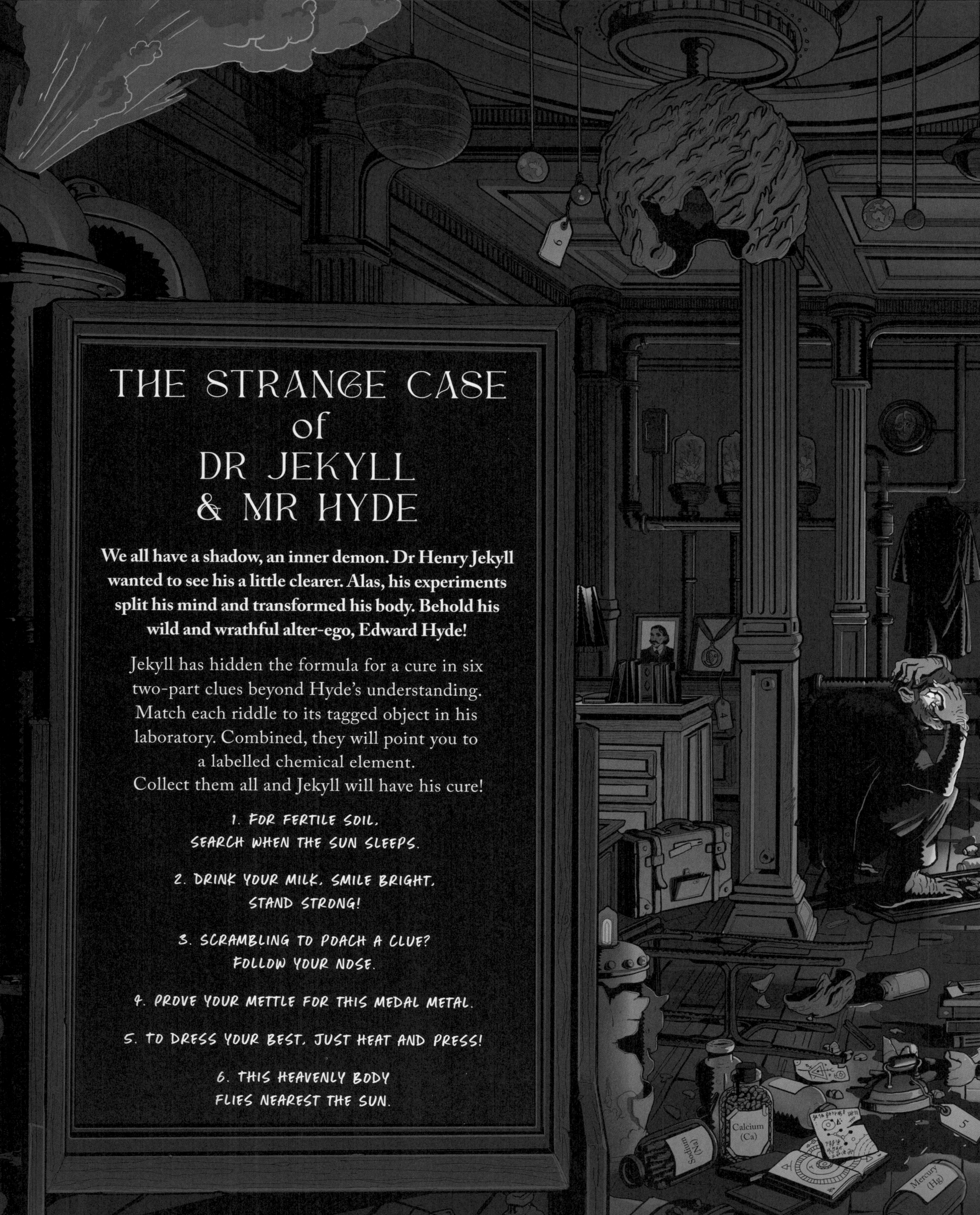

# THE STRANGE CASE of DR JEKYLL & MR HYDE

**We all have a shadow, an inner demon. Dr Henry Jekyll wanted to see his a little clearer. Alas, his experiments split his mind and transformed his body. Behold his wild and wrathful alter-ego, Edward Hyde!**

Jekyll has hidden the formula for a cure in six two-part clues beyond Hyde's understanding. Match each riddle to its tagged object in his laboratory. Combined, they will point you to a labelled chemical element. Collect them all and Jekyll will have his cure!

1. FOR FERTILE SOIL, SEARCH WHEN THE SUN SLEEPS.
2. DRINK YOUR MILK, SMILE BRIGHT, STAND STRONG!
3. SCRAMBLING TO POACH A CLUE? FOLLOW YOUR NOSE.
4. PROVE YOUR METTLE FOR THIS MEDAL METAL.
5. TO DRESS YOUR BEST, JUST HEAT AND PRESS!
6. THIS HEAVENLY BODY FLIES NEAREST THE SUN.

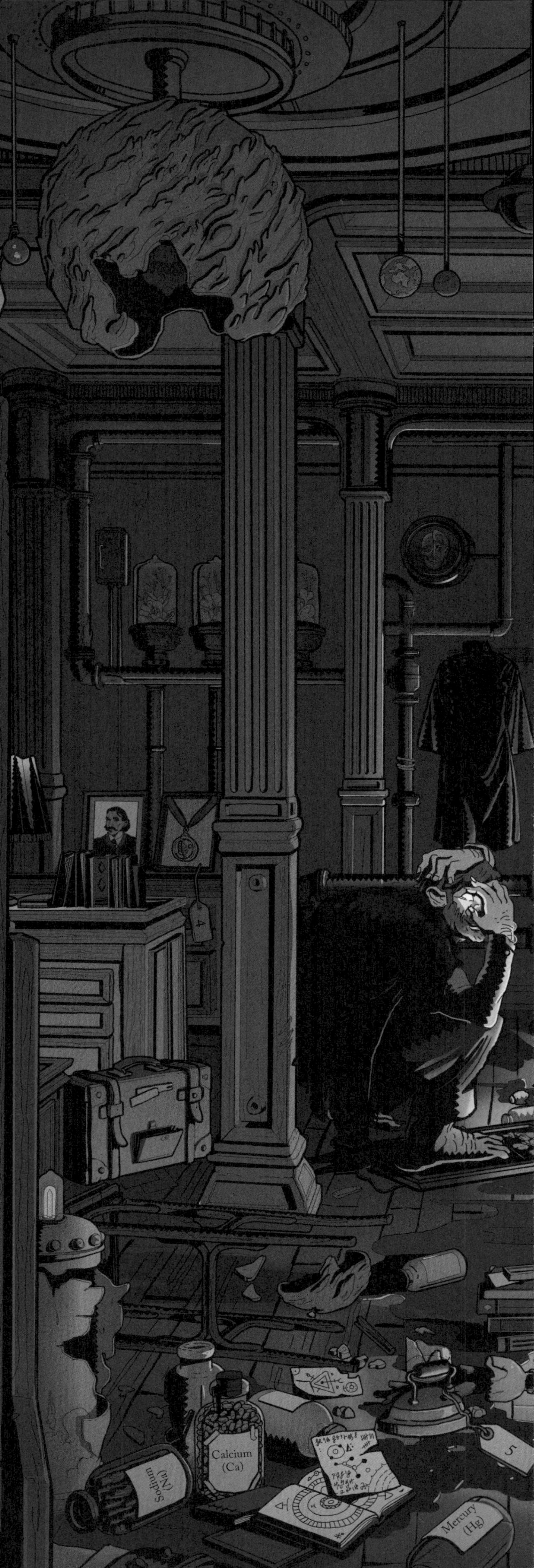
6
4
5
Calcium (Ca)
Sodium (Na)
Mercury (Hg)

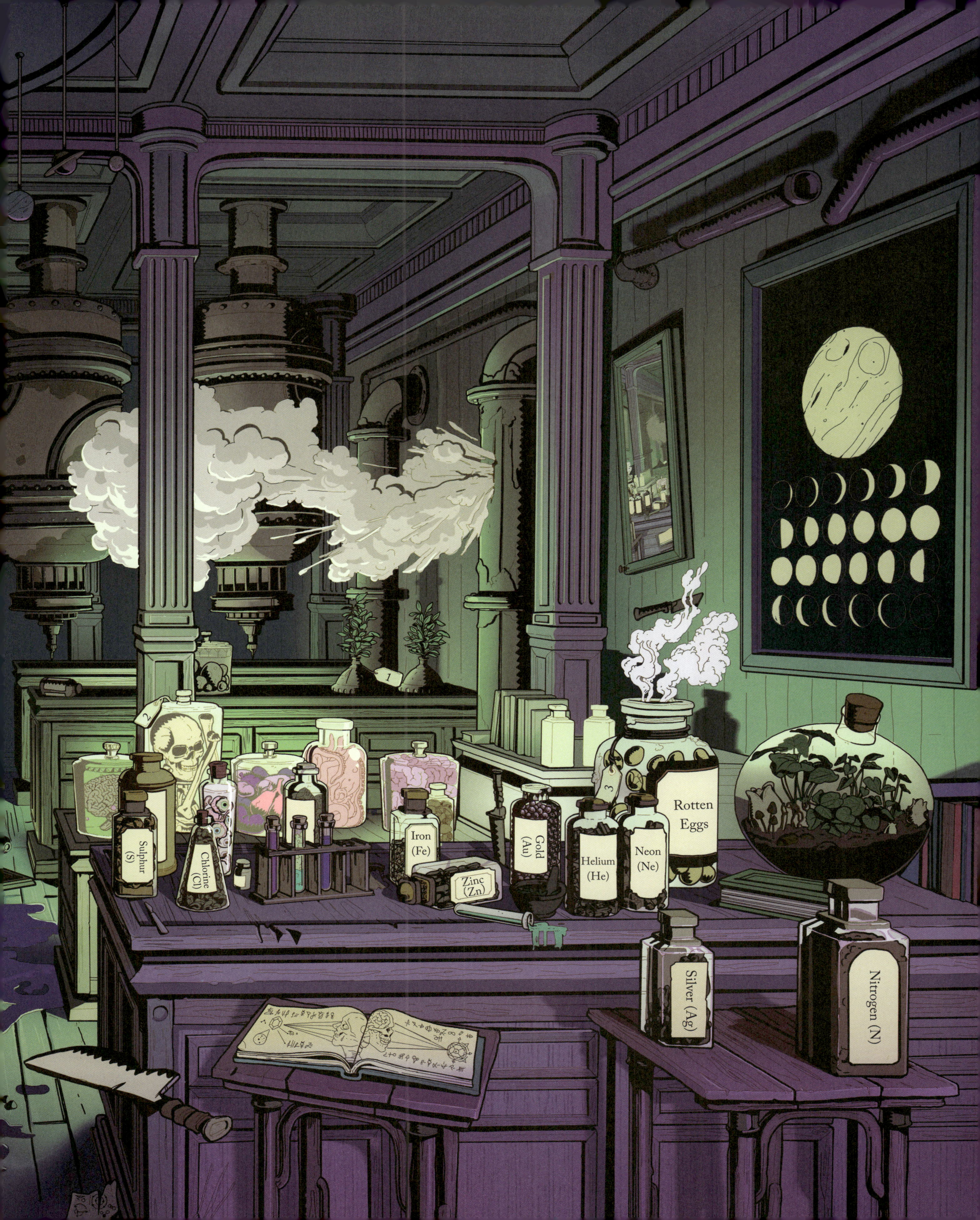

1
2
3
Sulphur (S)
Chlorine (Cl)
Iron (Fe)
Zinc (Zn)
Gold (Au)
Helium (He)
Neon (Ne)
Rotten Eggs
Silver (Ag)
Nitrogen (N)

# THE RAVEN

**One dreary midnight in Philadelphia, a widower weeps for his lost love. In his grief, he has summoned a demon – the Raven itself – to resurrect his lost Lenore. Little does he know that the Raven plans to inhabit her body…**

The Raven requires six heartfelt offerings from Lenore's life. The altar flames show their shape. Steal them back from the fiendish flock and thwart the demon's rise!

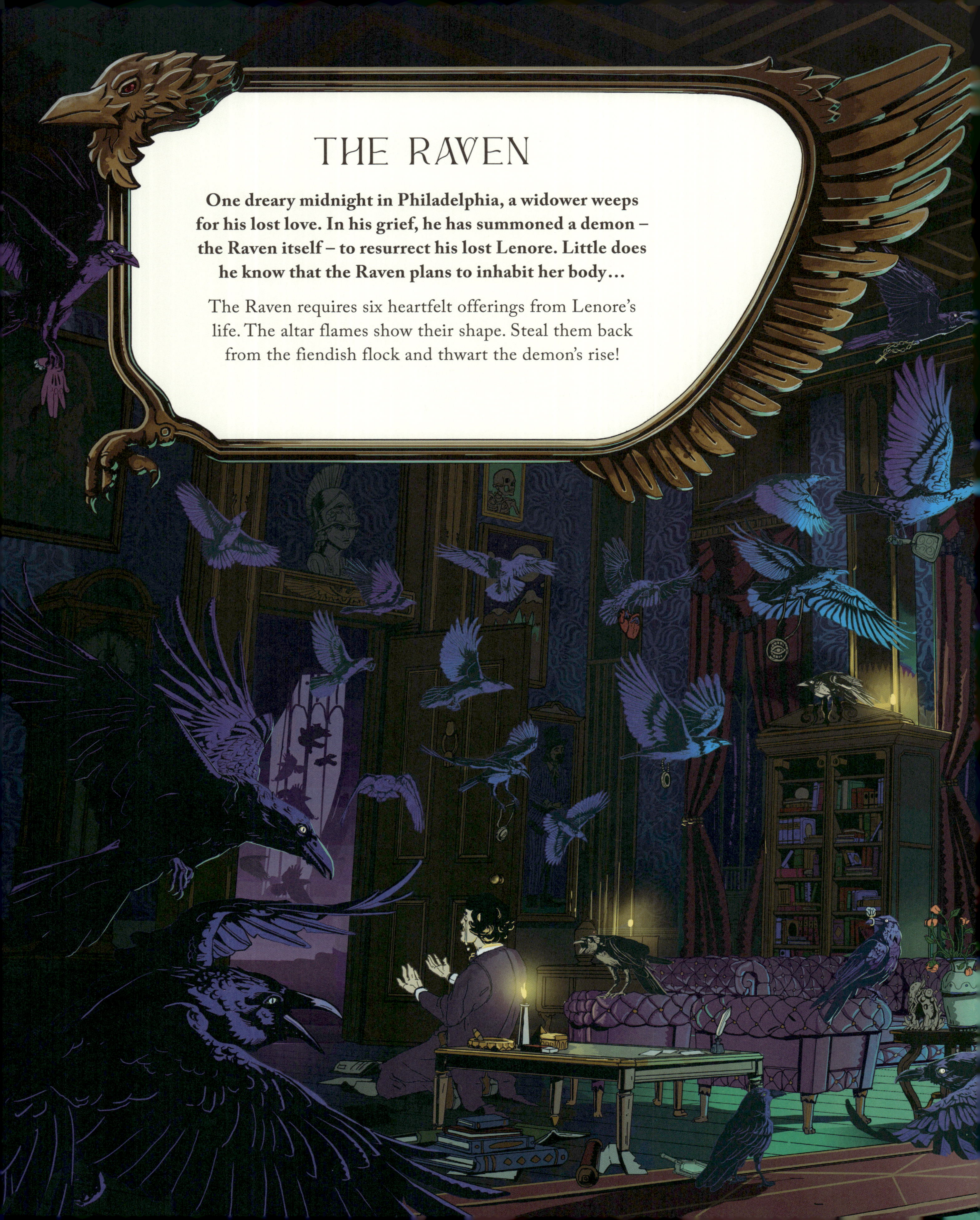

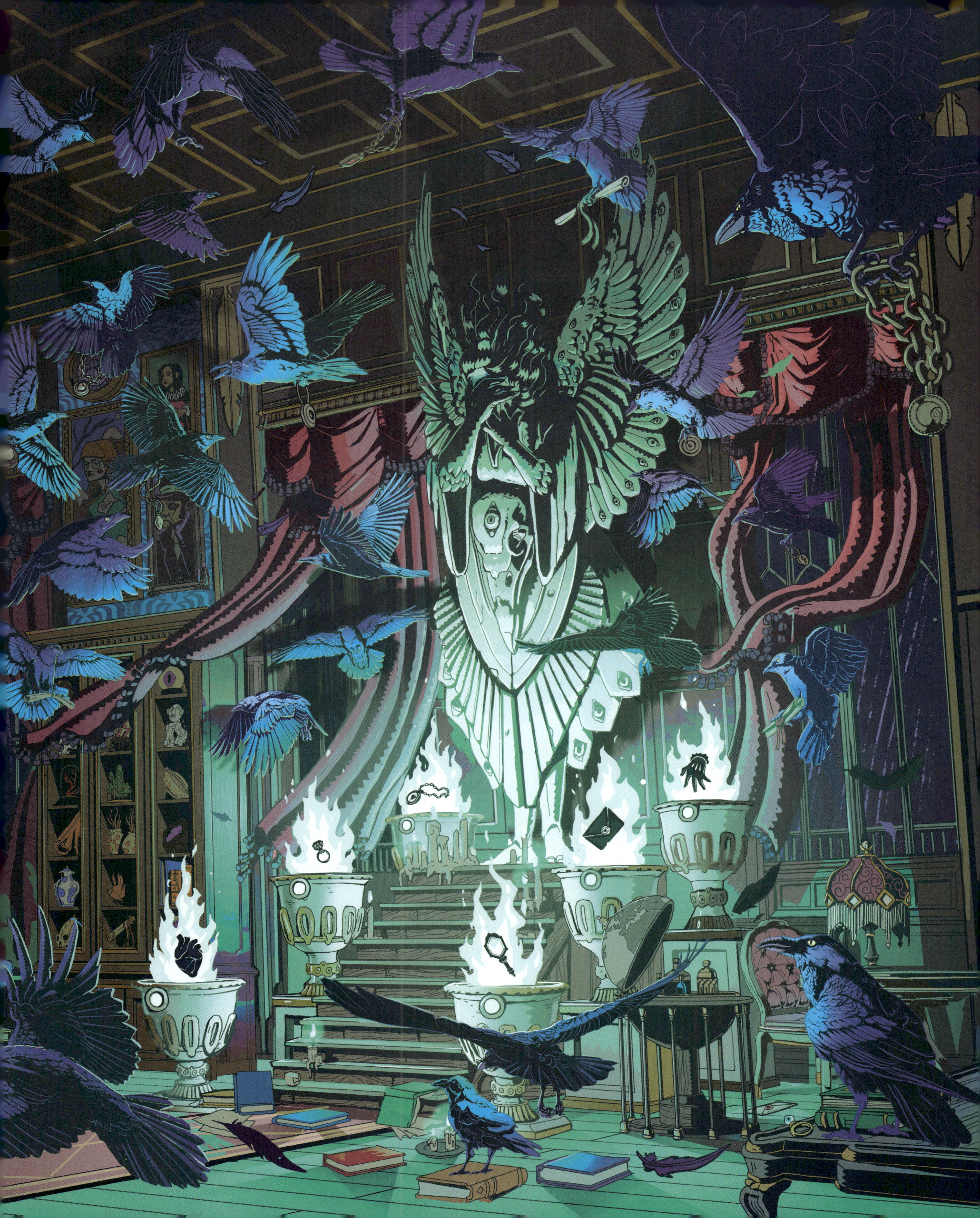

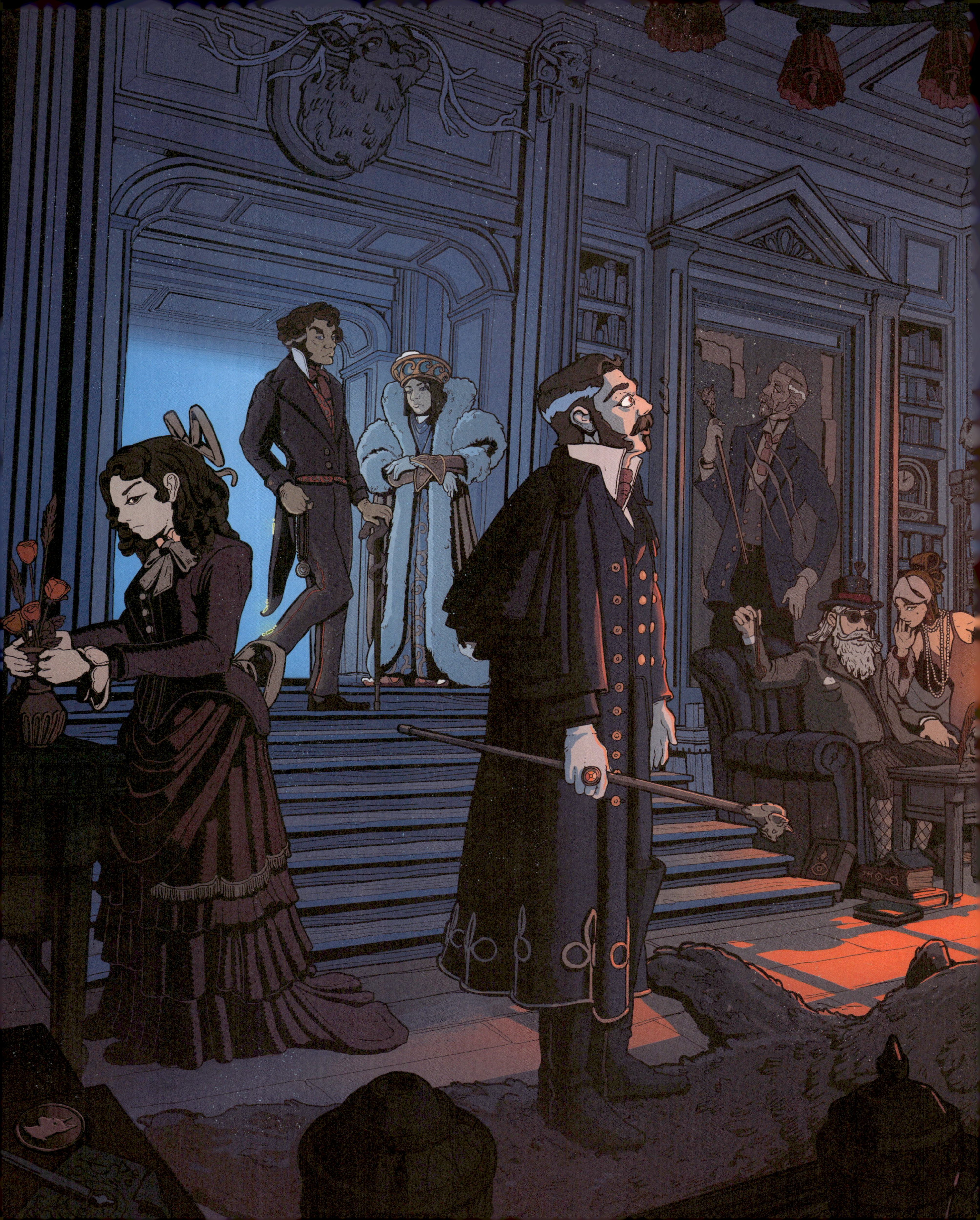

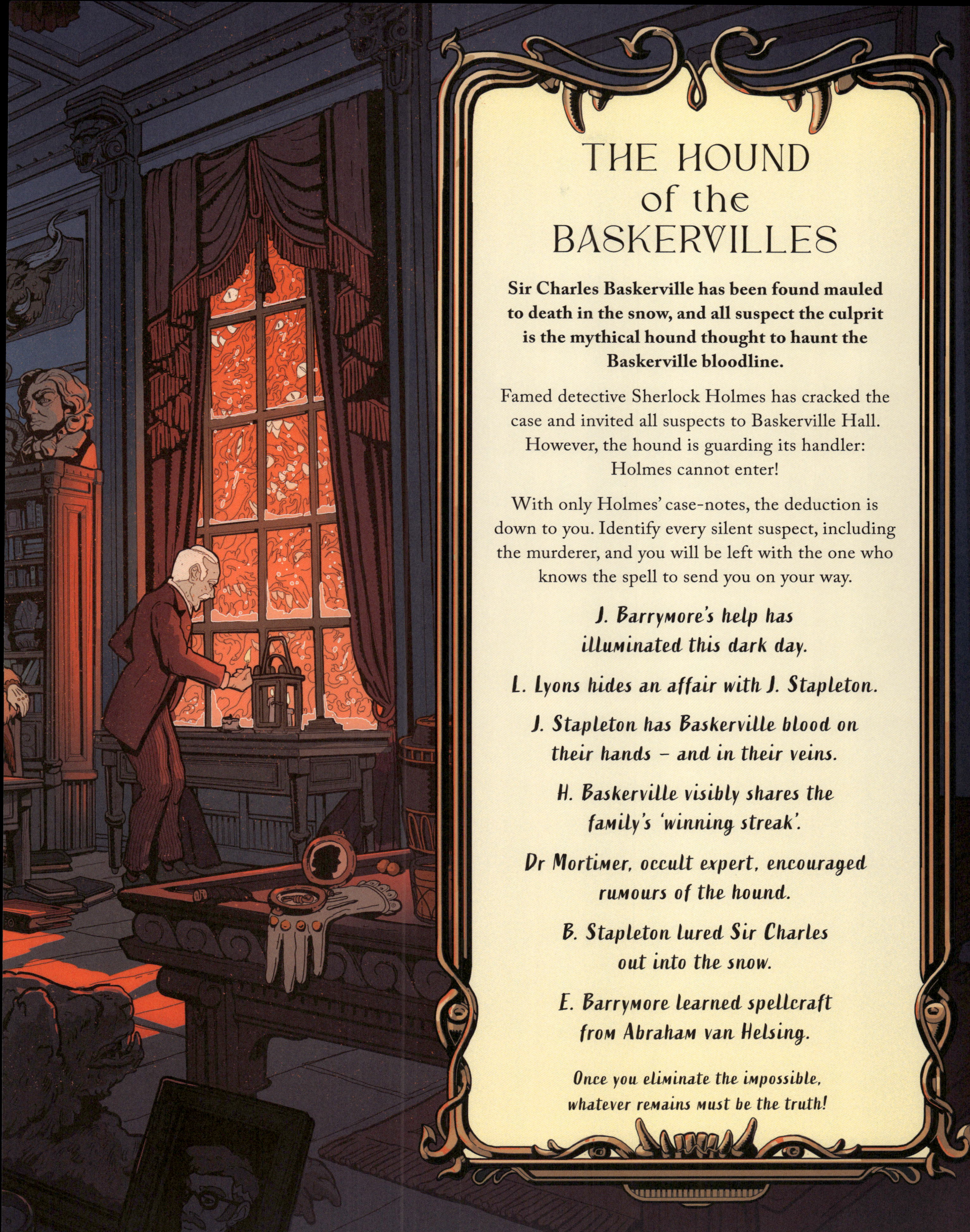

# THE HOUND of the BASKERVILLES

**Sir Charles Baskerville has been found mauled to death in the snow, and all suspect the culprit is the mythical hound thought to haunt the Baskerville bloodline.**

Famed detective Sherlock Holmes has cracked the case and invited all suspects to Baskerville Hall. However, the hound is guarding its handler: Holmes cannot enter!

With only Holmes' case-notes, the deduction is down to you. Identify every silent suspect, including the murderer, and you will be left with the one who knows the spell to send you on your way.

J. Barrymore's help has illuminated this dark day.

L. Lyons hides an affair with J. Stapleton.

J. Stapleton has Baskerville blood on their hands – and in their veins.

H. Baskerville visibly shares the family's 'winning streak'.

Dr Mortimer, occult expert, encouraged rumours of the hound.

B. Stapleton lured Sir Charles out into the snow.

E. Barrymore learned spellcraft from Abraham van Helsing.

*Once you eliminate the impossible, whatever remains must be the truth!*

# SLEEPY HOLLOW

**Many long years ago, this Hessian soldier tormented the town of Sleepy Hollow until a cannonball blew his head off. The townspeople refused to bury the monster, instead hiding his parts around the land to ensure he never rests. Now, once a year, he returns for his revenge!**

Ichabod Crane faced him down, but could not defeat him. Ride Crane's horse, Gunpowder, along the paths, and hunt for the Horseman's:

**skeletal legs, arms, torso, two pistols, battle-axe, flag, sword and skull.**

Once found, burn the galloping ghoul's remains in the bonfire to dismount him for good.

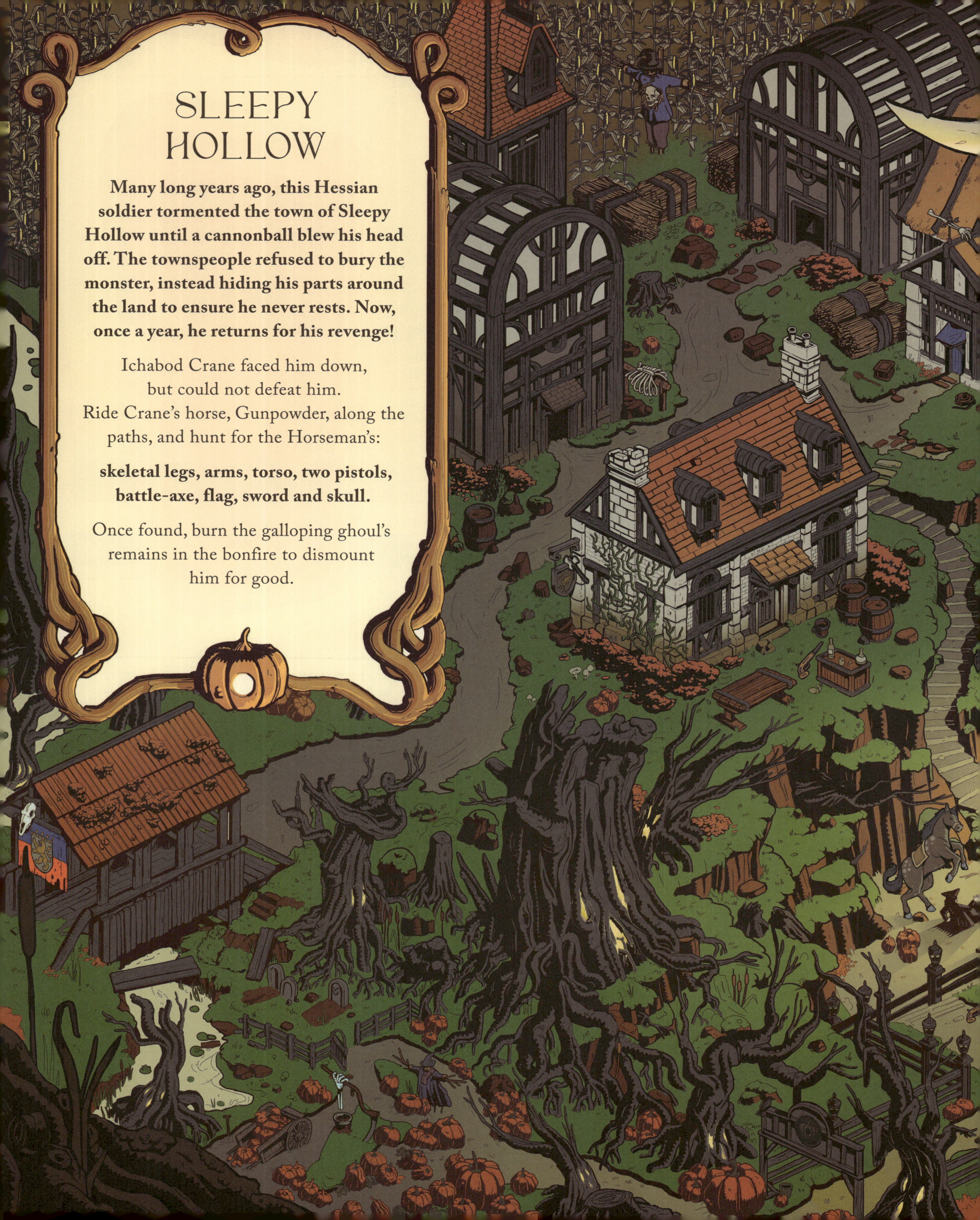

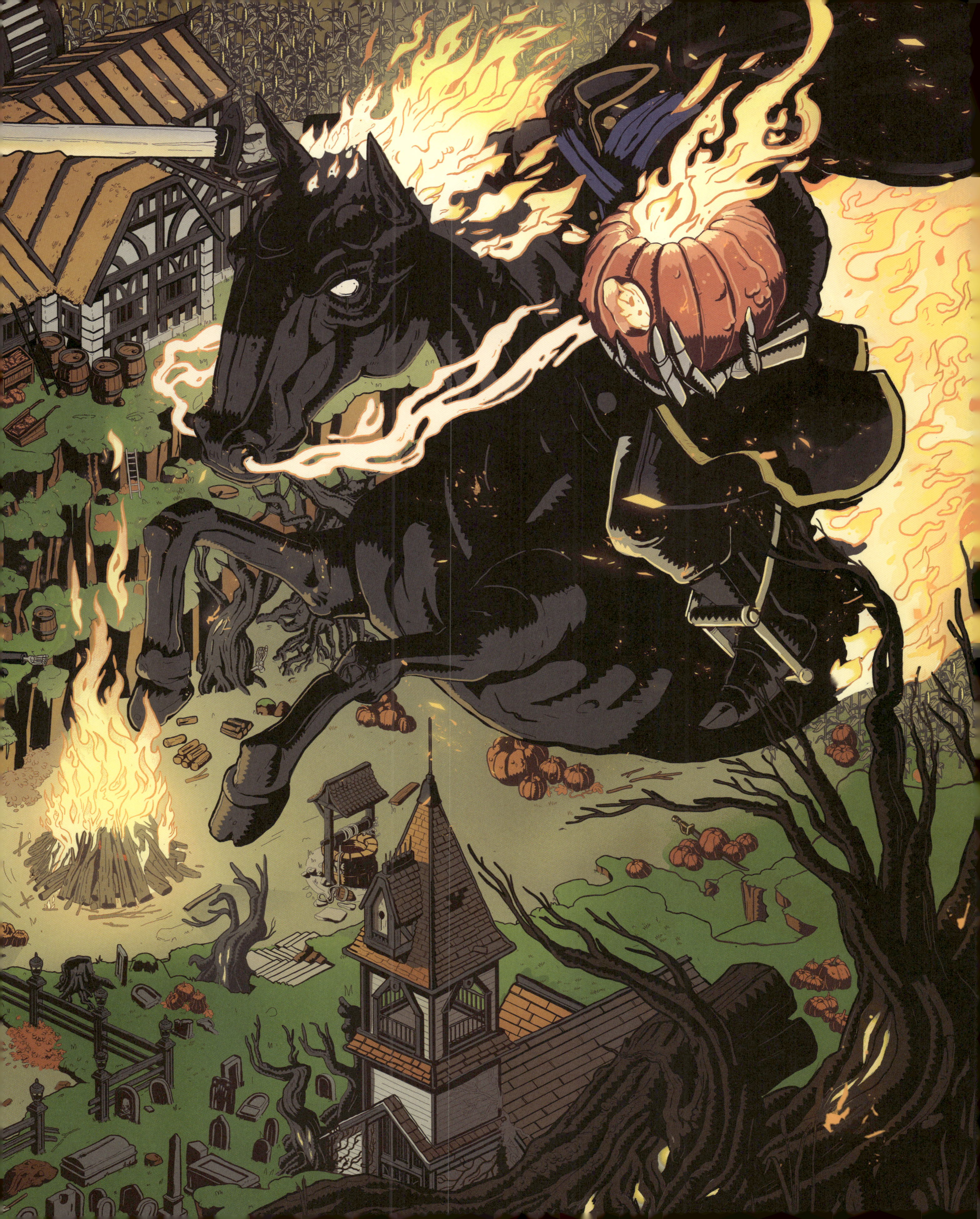

# THE YELLOW WALLPAPER

**Imprisoned by her own husband, this woman fights for escape, but even with her eyes covered, she knows she's not locked in here alone. Like mould to dirt, her husband's cruelty has summoned a demon into the wallpaper.**

Where her husband locked one door and hid one key, the demon has added four locks, hundreds more keys, and has stretched her prison into strange dimensions.

Find the true keys by matching them to those sketched below, and free the both of you!

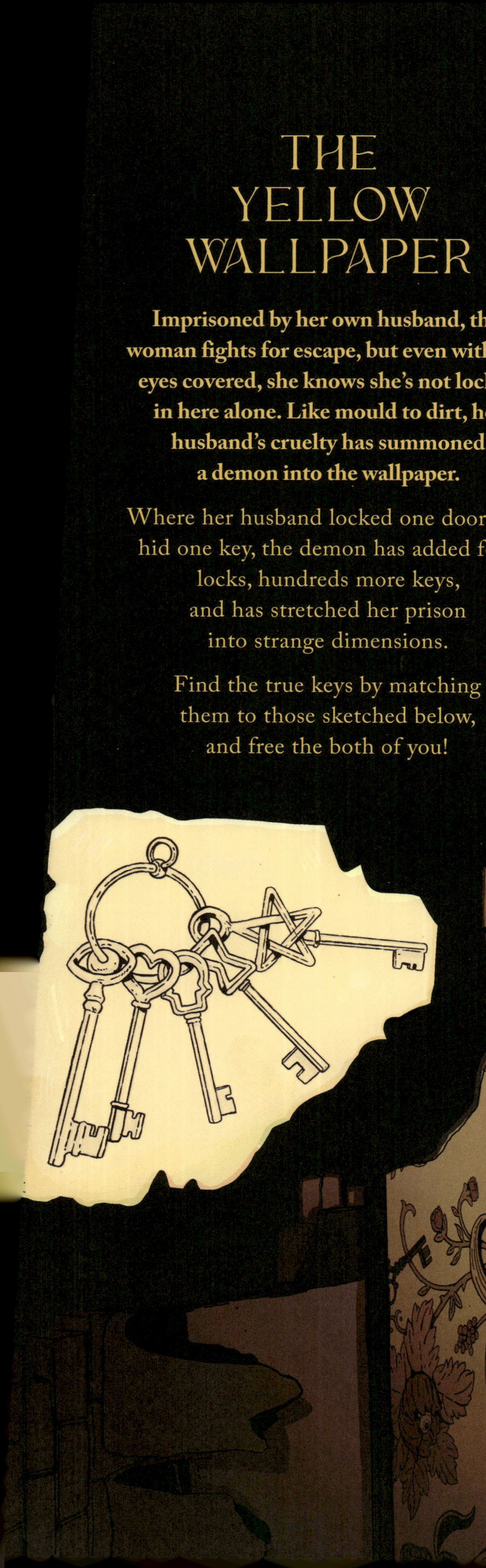

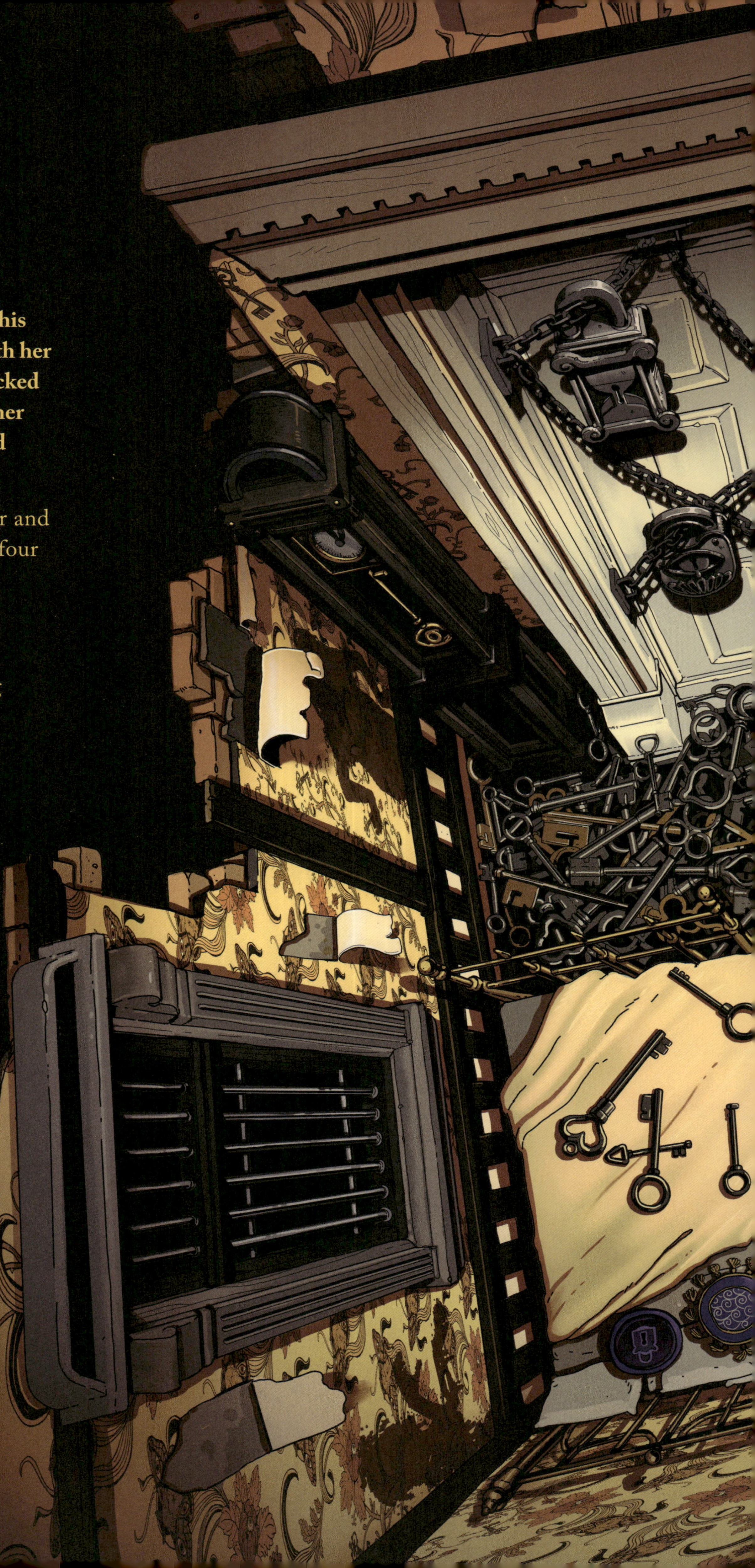

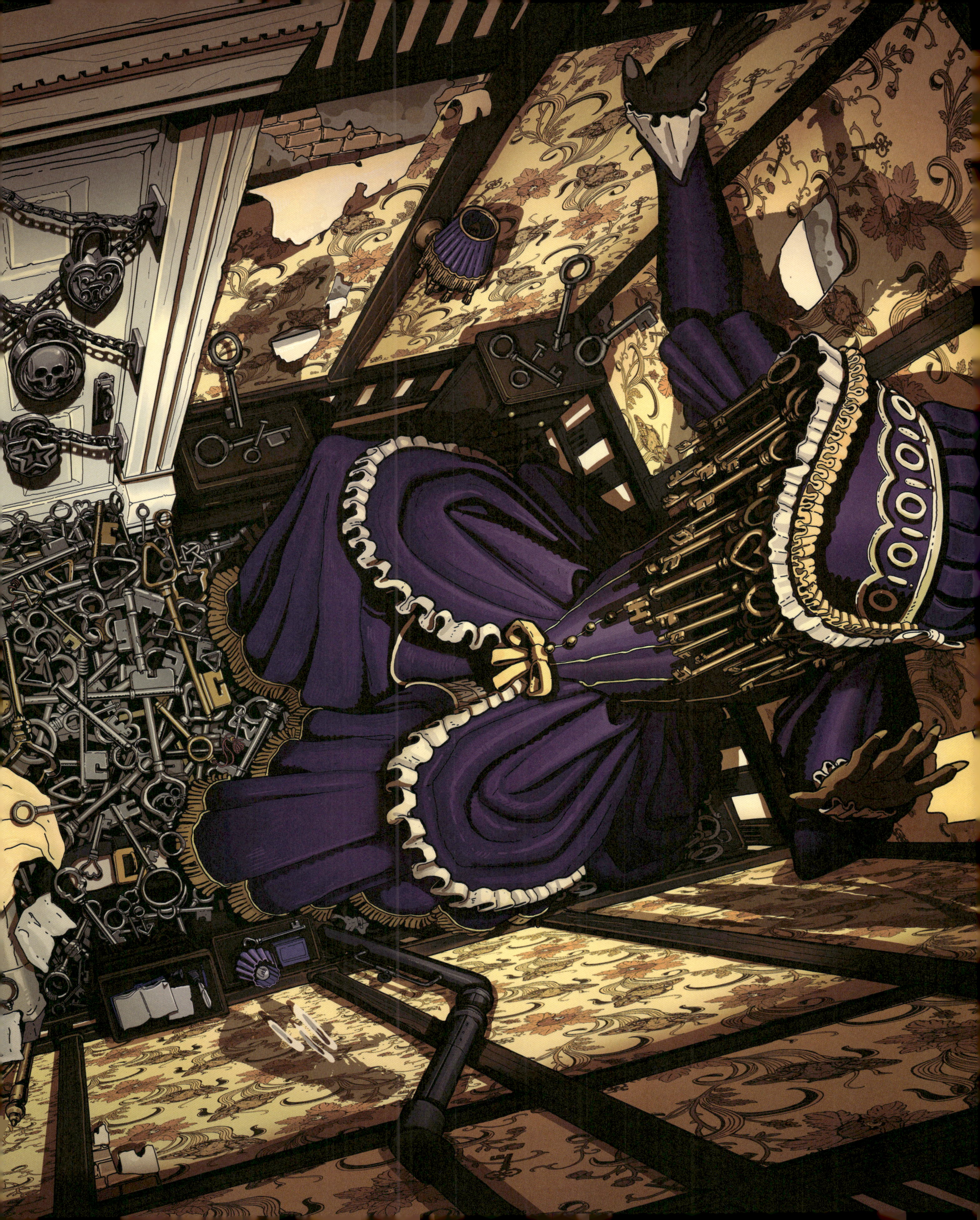

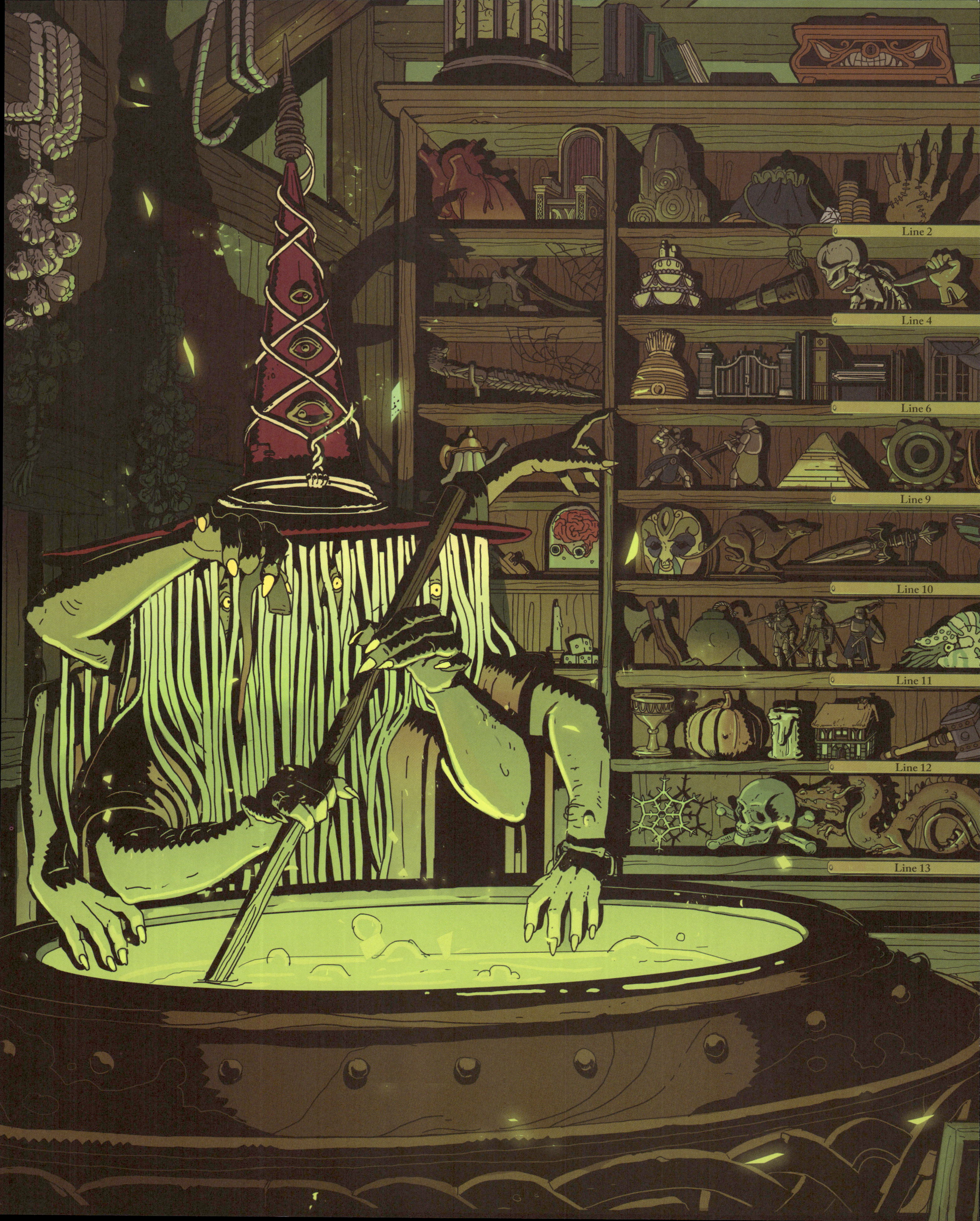
Line 2
Line 4
Line 6
Line 9
Line 10
Line 11
Line 12
Line 13

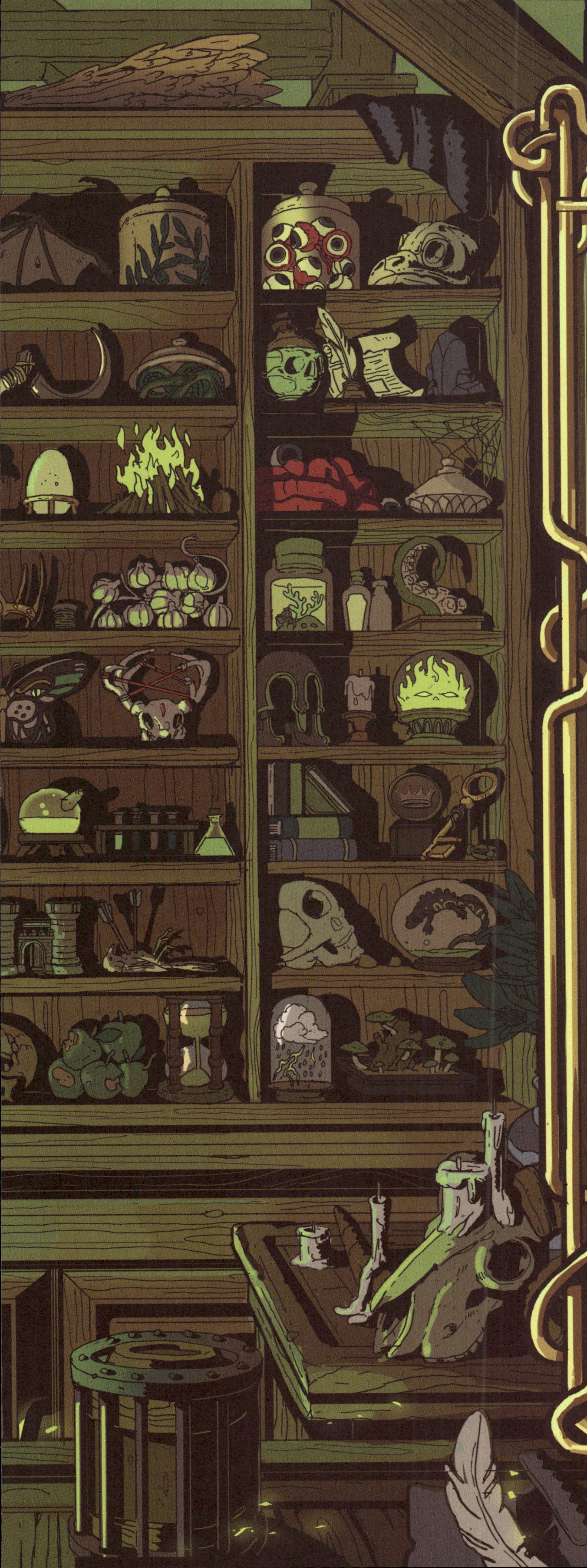

# MACBETH

**Hekate's three witches stir up only toil and trouble! Their latest song celebrates their infamous corruption of Macbeth.**

Together with his wife, the witches persuaded proud warrior Macbeth to murder King Duncan and steal the Scottish throne. When his friend Banquo grew suspicious, Macbeth killed him, too. At last, he fell at Dunsinane Castle to an army gathered by Duncan's sons, who stormed his stronghold camouflaged as trees.

Fill each silence in their song. Choose an item from the top shelf for the first gap, working down to Macbeth's final fate. Choose wrong, and you will share it!

*Ah, noble Macbeth – till we led him astray,*
*Our prophecies promising him Scotland's __*
*At the cost of King Duncan's trust to betray:*
*__ most foul, for a land of his own.*

*We promised him harm from no man woman-born*
*Nor death till the woodland stalks up to his __,*
*So Macbeth hosts fair Duncan, loyalties torn,*
*But his Lady spurs him to his murderous fate.*

*Lo, blood begets blood: Macbeth wins the __,*
*Yet guilt turns his __ on Banquo, old friend.*
*Duncan's heirs gather help: see their __ bring down*
*That usurper's __, our stage for the end.*

*Now __ seeks Macbeth, rightful, wrongful, insane,*
*Hidden and haunted in dark Dunsinane.*

# THE KING in YELLOW

**Even Dracula fears the tattered god Hastur, King in Yellow, ruler of lost Carcosa. The cosmic wellspring of the weird, Carcosa feeds like a fungus on our world, secret and unseeable** ***…until the King's gaze turns to you!***

Hastur works his influence through his regal rune – pictured below. Find all thirteen instances of the rune woven between his land and our own, prove your sight worthy of his work, and the King may let you leave.

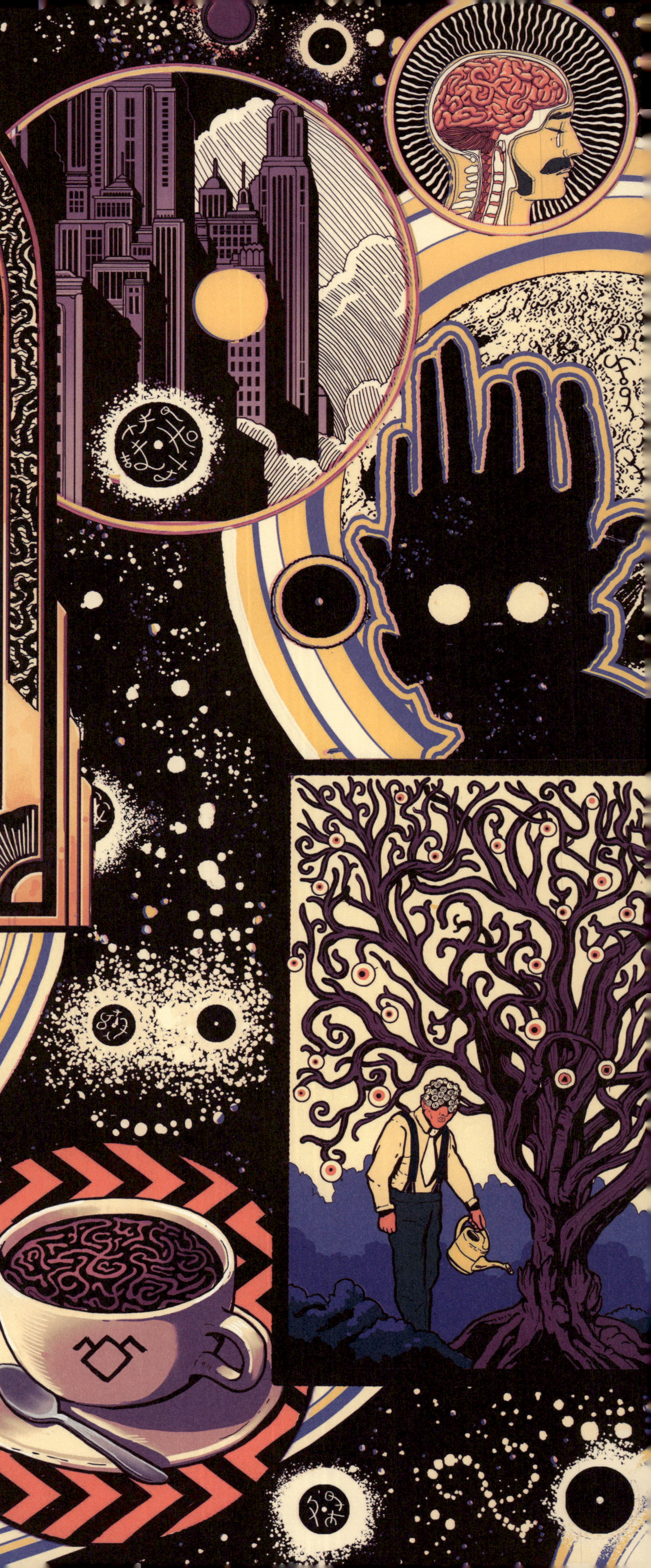

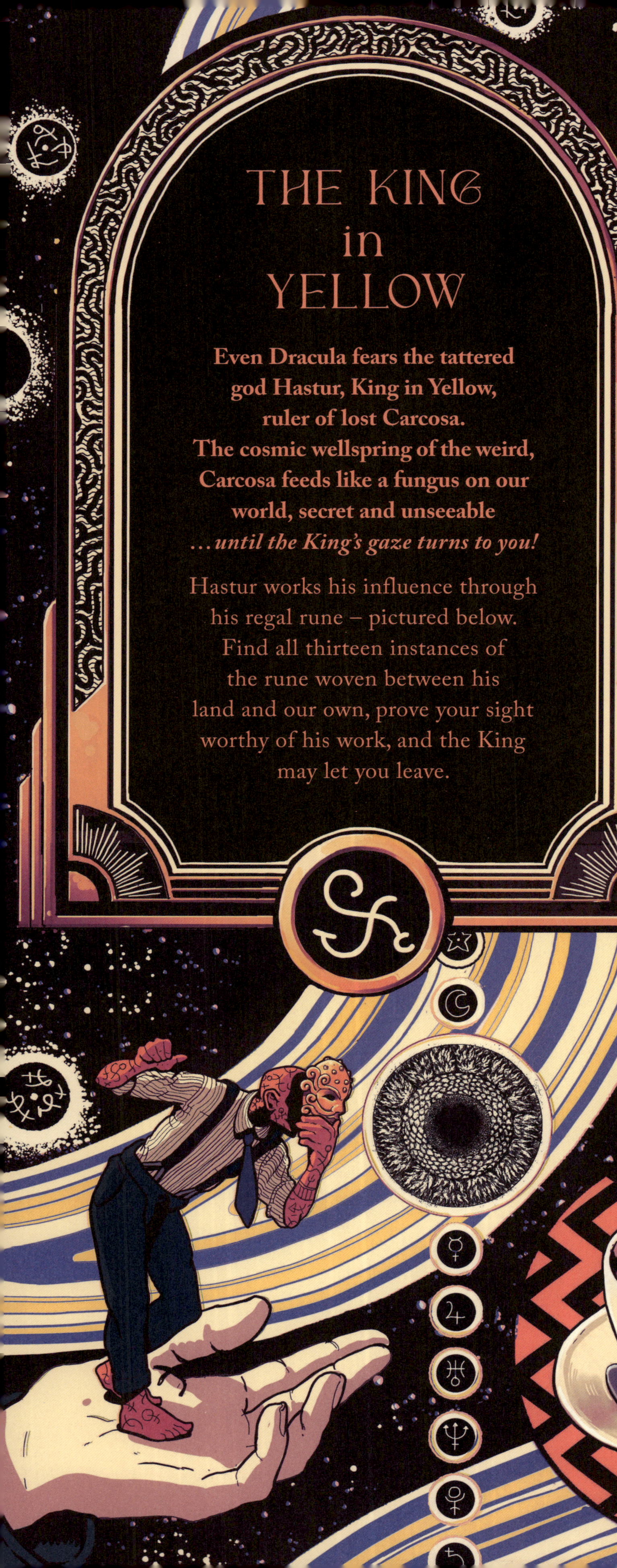

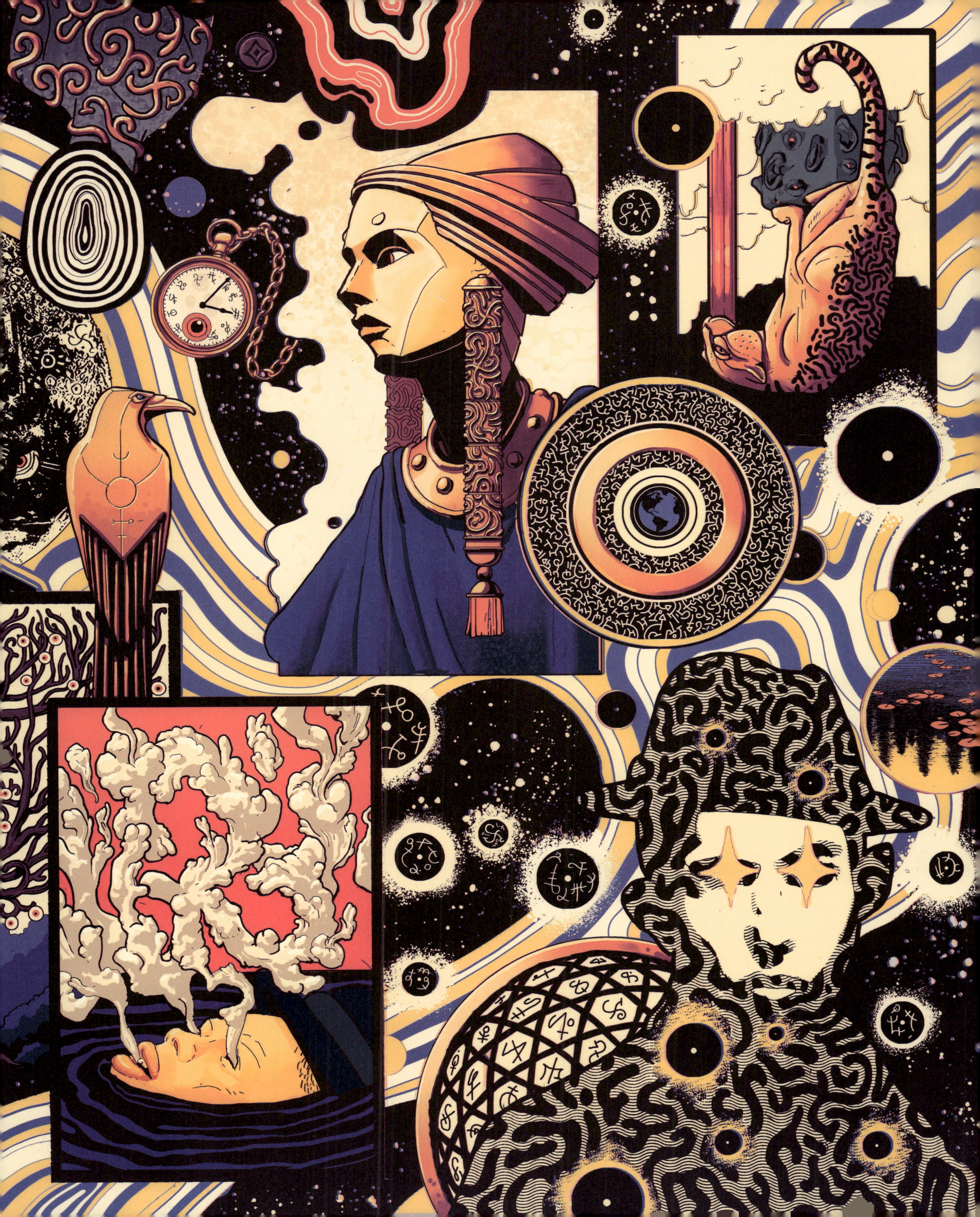

# THE PHANTOM of the OPERA

Mad with unrequited love for Christine Daaé, soprano of the Palais Garnier Opera House, the masked murderer known as the Phantom has set the place ablaze with a sabotaged chandelier, kidnapped Christine, and escaped in the chaos to his underground lair!

The Phantom has trapped Christine in a cage secured with five musical locks. To free her, he demands to hear his work played on his piano...

Note the colours shared between the five locks around the cage and the five piano keys. The Phantom has scattered roses of these same colours all over his lair. Count every rose of each lock colour, then play their corresponding piano keys: the colour with the fewest roses first, and then up to the colour with the most.

*Beware: one wrong note and it's curtains for you both!*

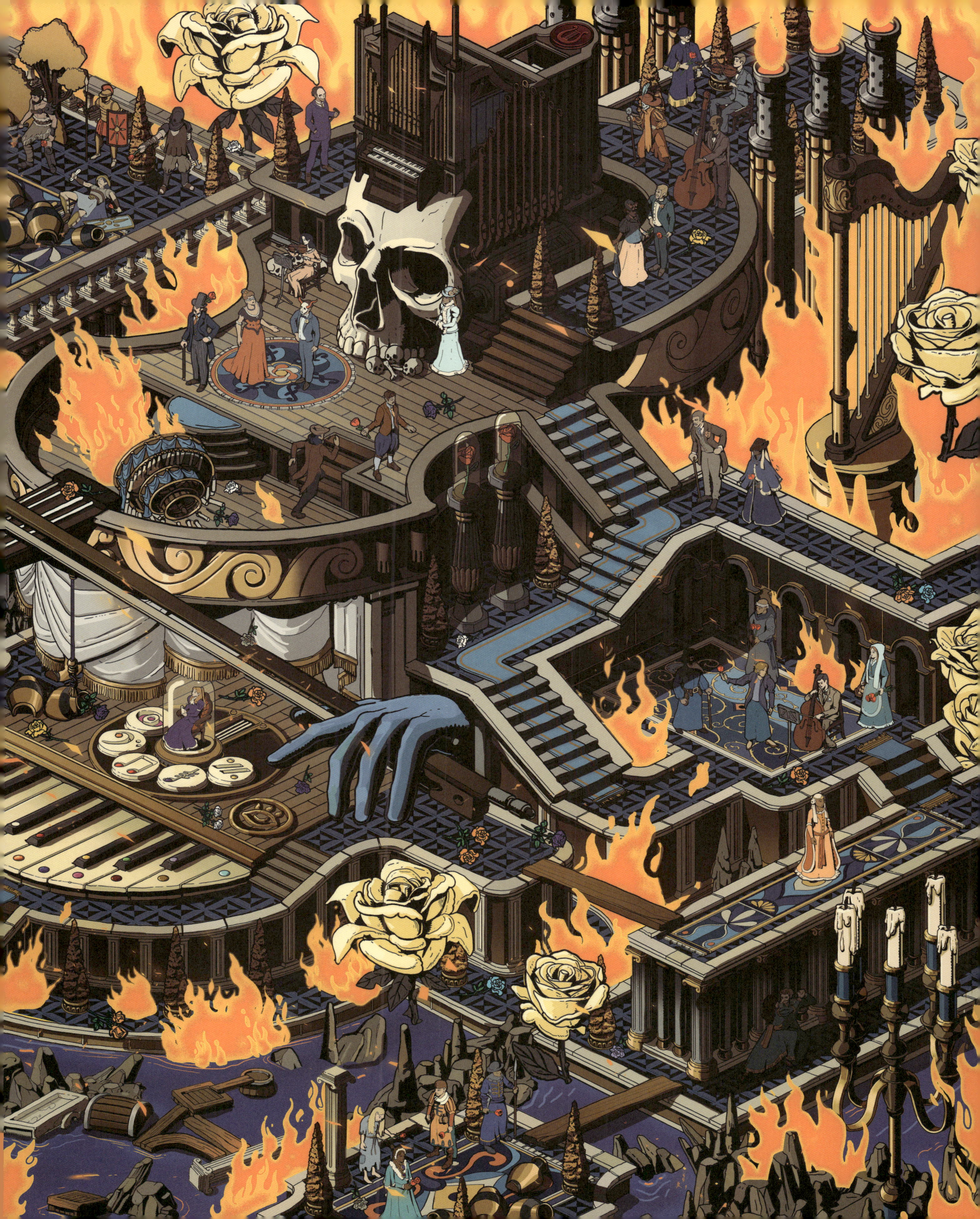

# FRANKENSTEIN

**Victor Frankenstein has built a body from the dead. With a strike of lightning this poor creature may wake.**

With the storm fast on the wind, Victor will pay any price for assistance finishing his creature – for instance, letting you leave his lab alive. On the right is a list of parts he needs to finish the grisly creation.

Take care to use only flawless pieces: no breaks, no diseases, and a correct fit. If you ruin his work with an injured or rotten part, he'll take a fresh replacement from you!

A. A Heart
B. A Left Hand
C. A Pair of Ears
D. A Right Foot
E. Matching Eyes
F. Four Teeth
G. A Pair of Lungs
H. One Forearm Bone
I. A Spine
J. A Brain
K. A Tongue

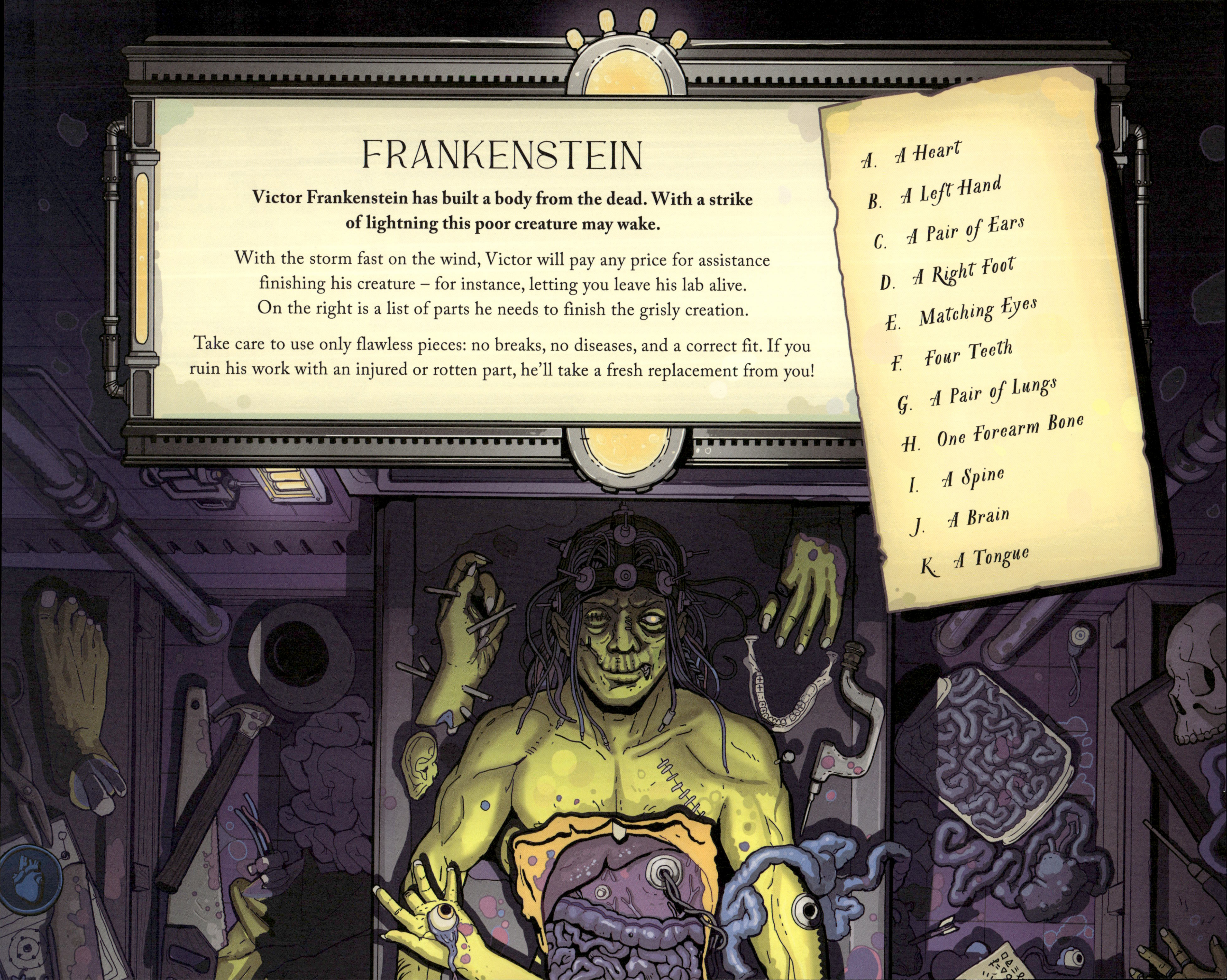

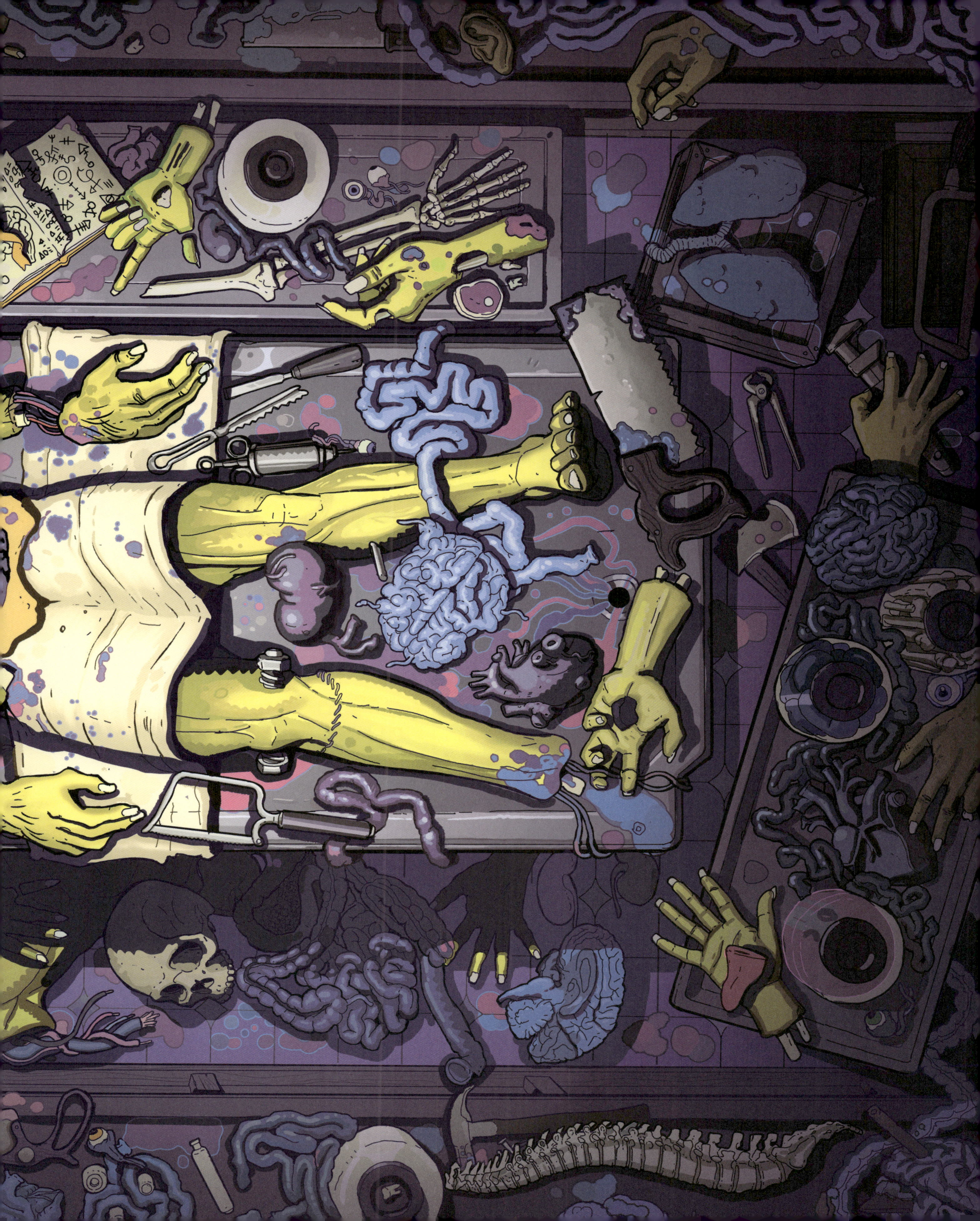

# THE INVISIBLE MAN

**Doctor Griffin formulated a chemical to turn himself invisible, but lacked Jekyll's talent for cures. Losing sight of his body (and mind), Griffin terrorises the market town of Iping with invisible acts of violence.**

To stop Griffin's rampage, you must create an unwashable dye unique in colour and potency. Each store contains a different ingredient – note my illustrations. But beware: wherever you go, Griffin will be hiding! Find him, and he'll flee to the next store. Collect the ingredients, shake them up, and a single splash will halt the reign of the Invisible Man!

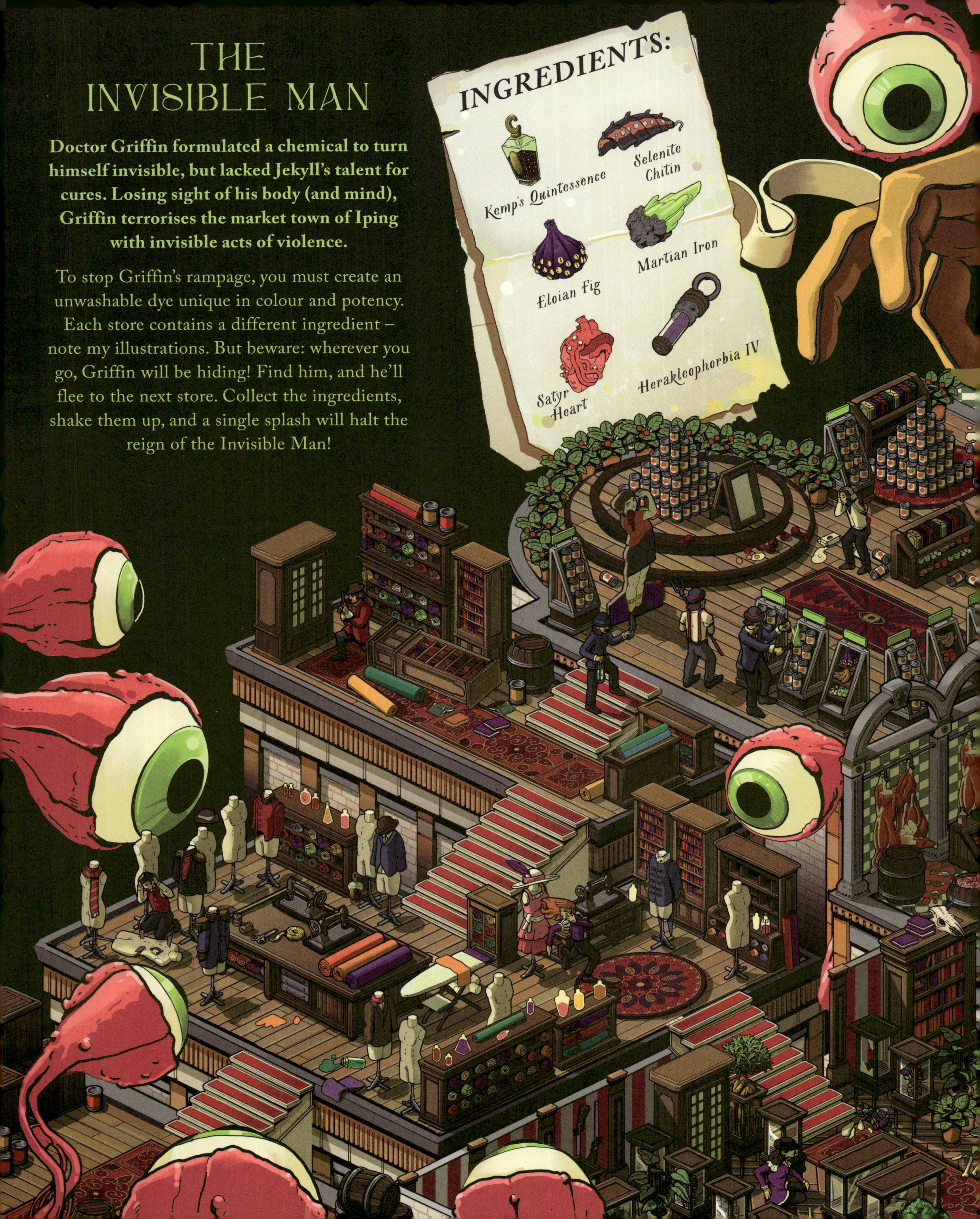

INGREDIENTS:
Kemp's Quintessence
Selenite Chitin
Eloian Fig
Martian Iron
Satyr Heart
Herakleophorbia IV

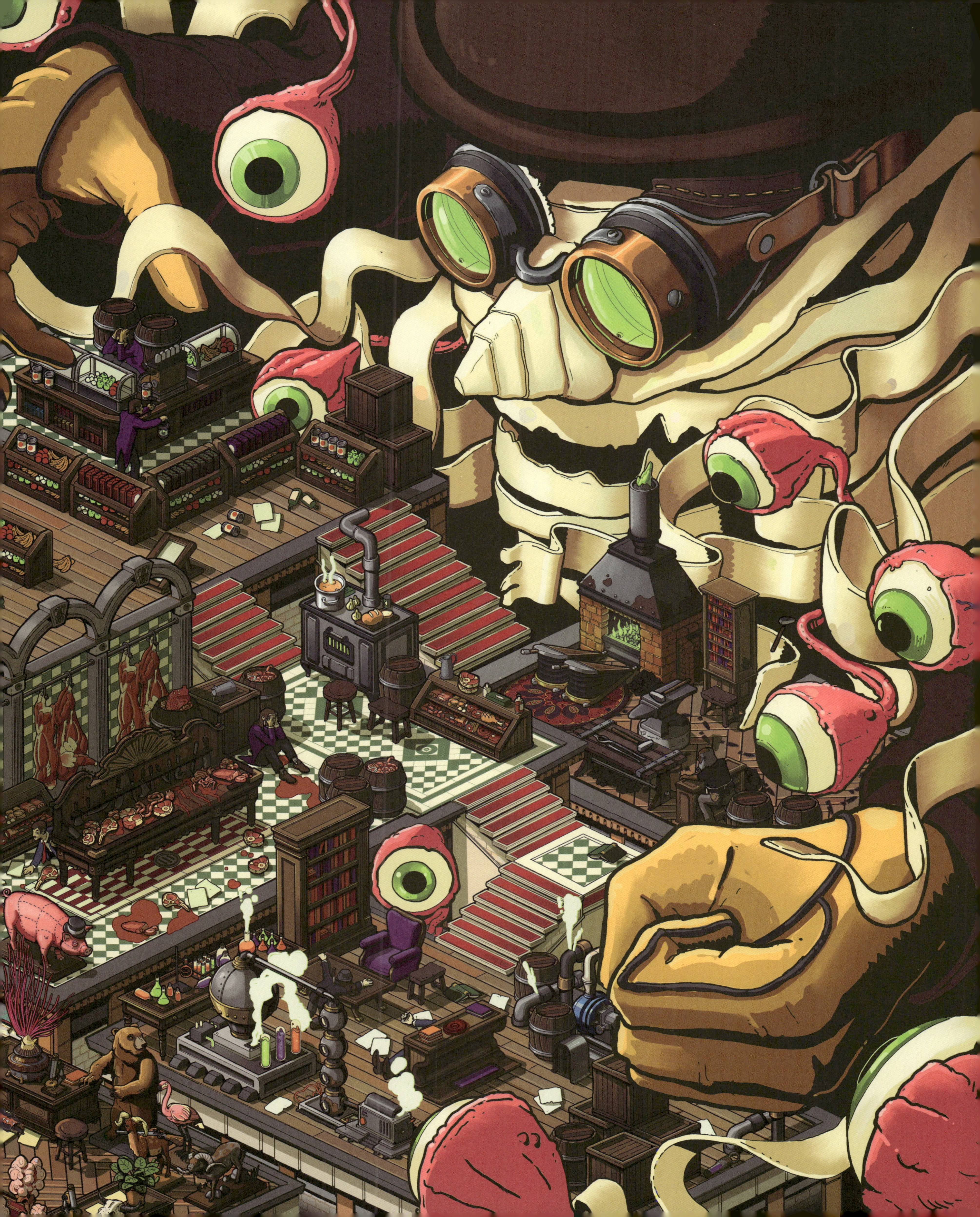

# THE PICTURE of DORIAN GRAY

**Welcome to the home of Dorian Gray, the man who proves that beauty is only skin deep. Binding his soul into his own portrait, Gray's body remains forever young and cherubic, while his picture withers and rots.**

After decades of debauchery, Gray's dread secret is out – but he knows where it went and how to stop its spread. All six socialites who learned the truth have received invitations to this masquerade…

To ensure their silence, Gray has ordered six of his acolytes to re-enact his previous crimes and murder them. Examine his portrait, then figure out who is truly dressed to kill – or prepare to take your last dance!

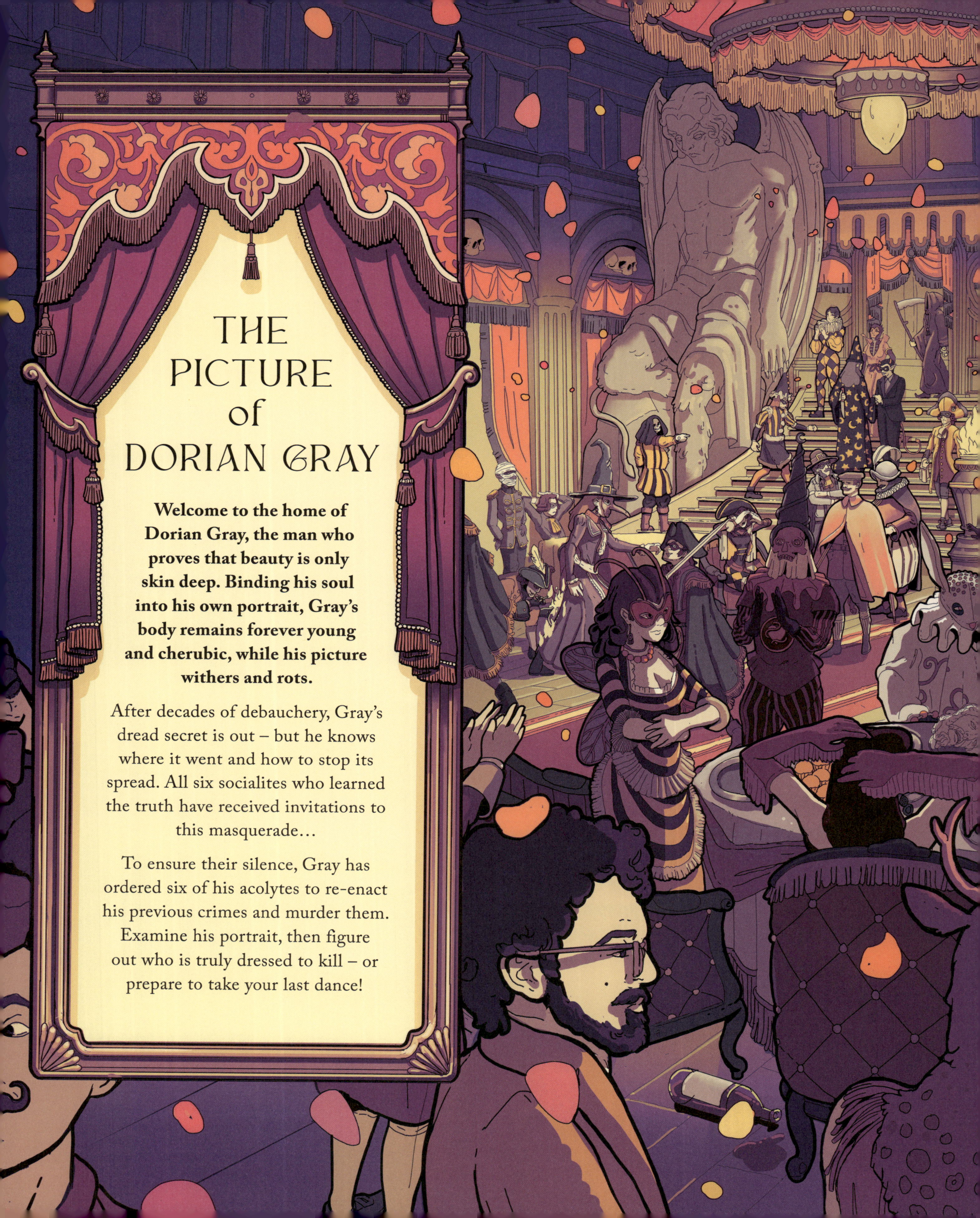

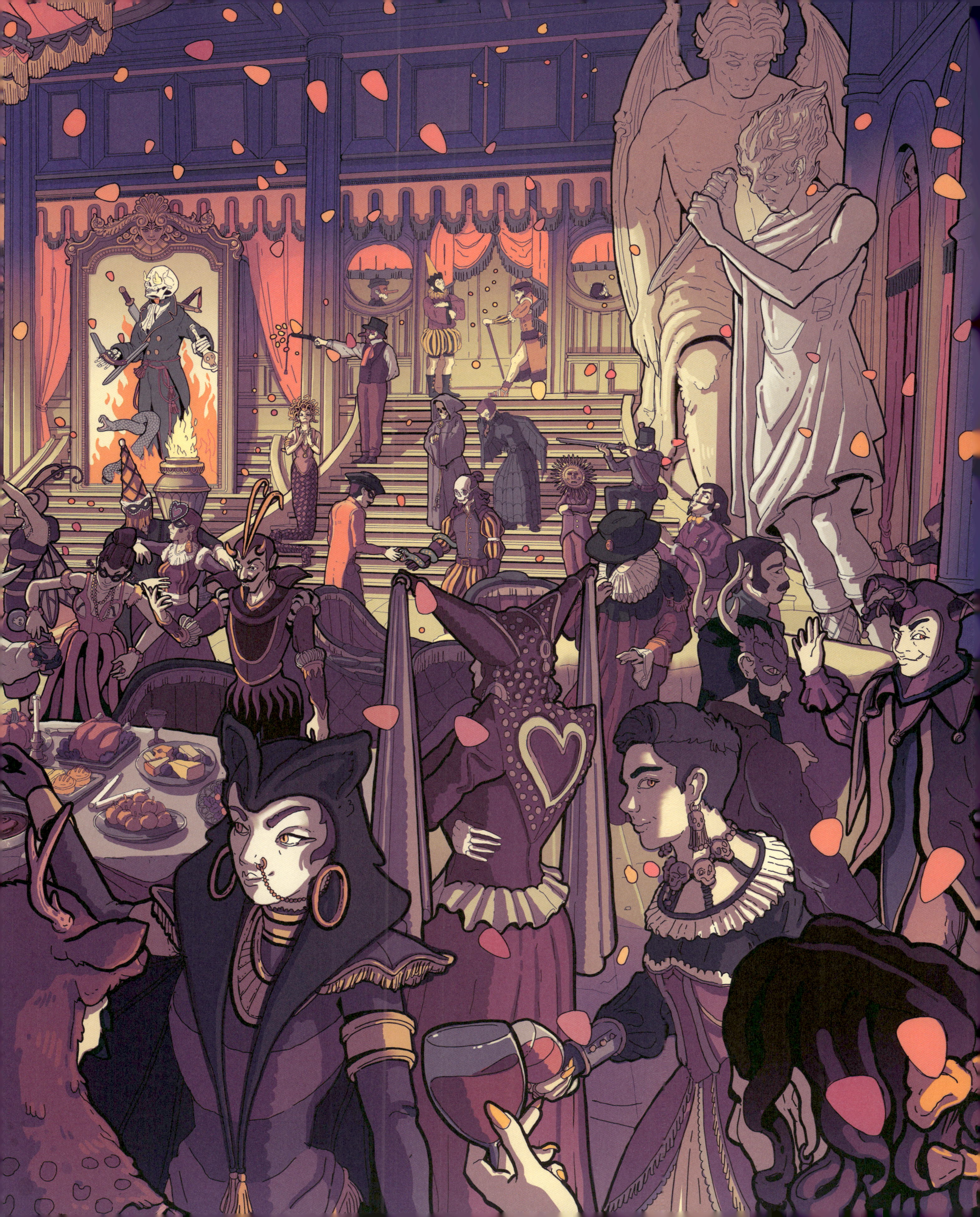

# DR FAUSTUS

**After a dastardly deal with the demon Mephistopheles, Johann Faustus enjoyed ten years of magic. The price?** ***His eternal soul.***

Faustus has just one trick left to escape his deal: feed another soul to Hell!

With the last of his magic, he will mirror himself enough to confuse the demon. Reveal the true Faustus to Mephistopheles and the grateful demon will send you out to freedom.

*Mind the details:*
Faustus has **tattooed his hand** and is never seen without his **gemstone**, his **pendant**, and his **serpent**.

*Fail, and Faustus' fiery fate is yours!*

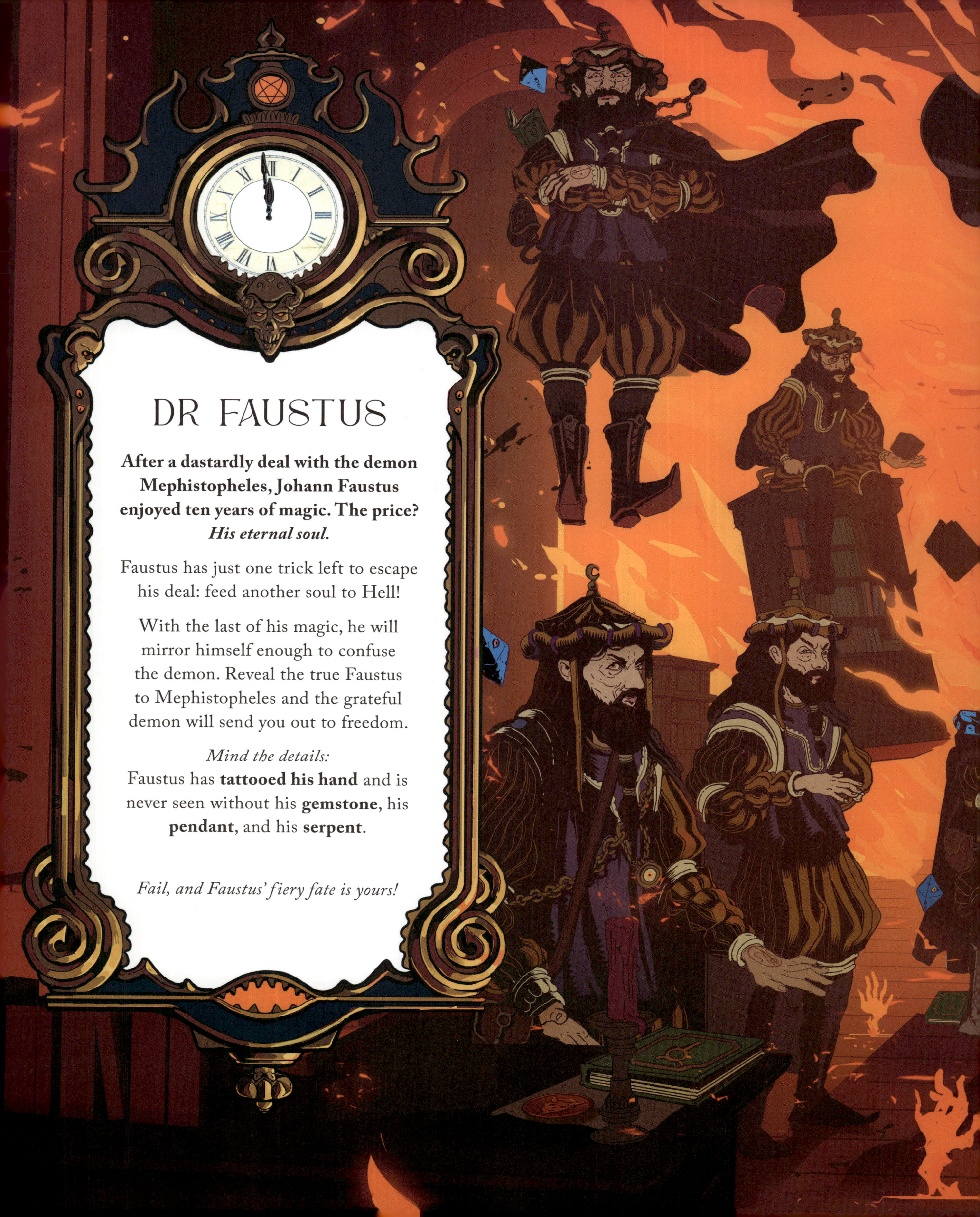

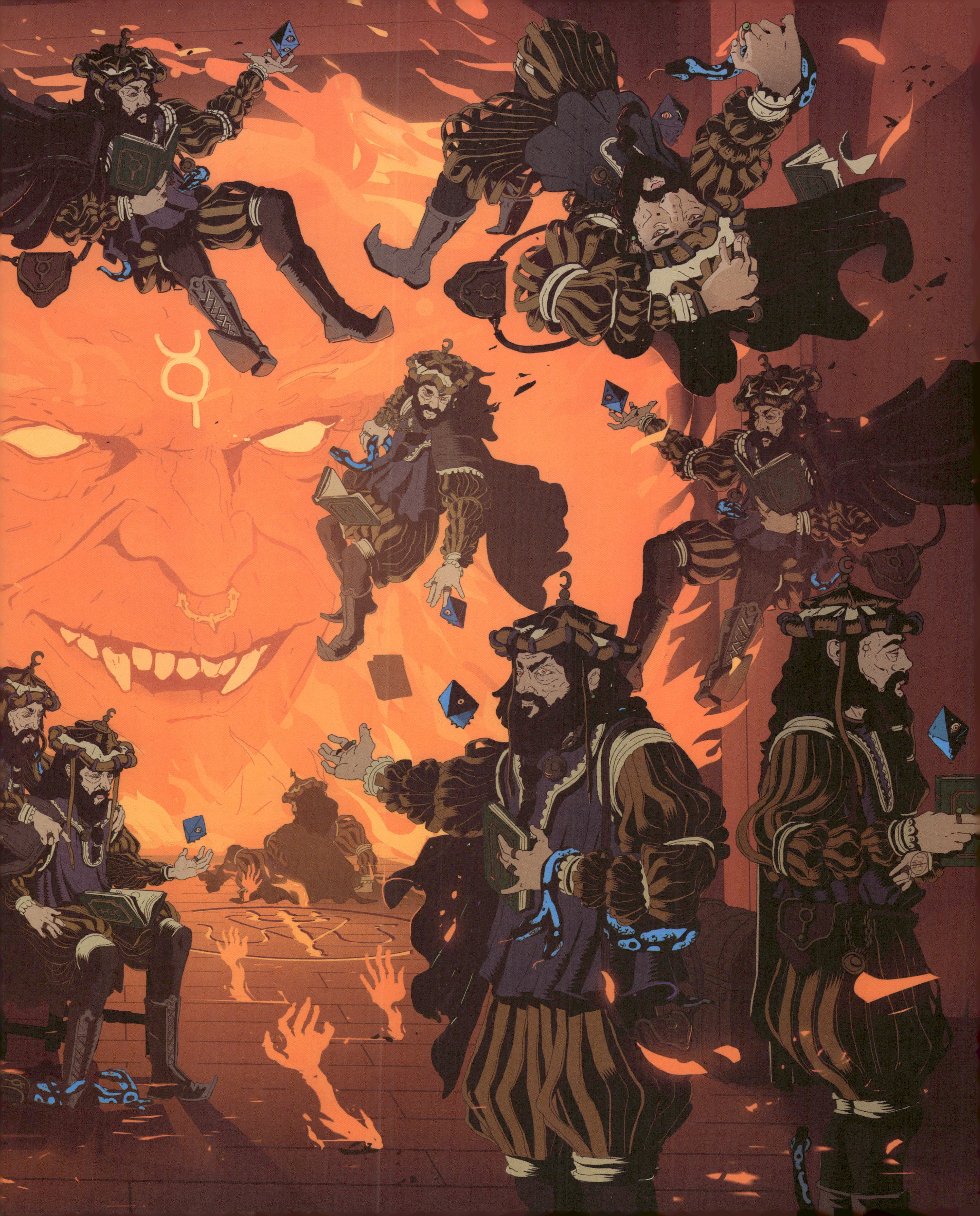

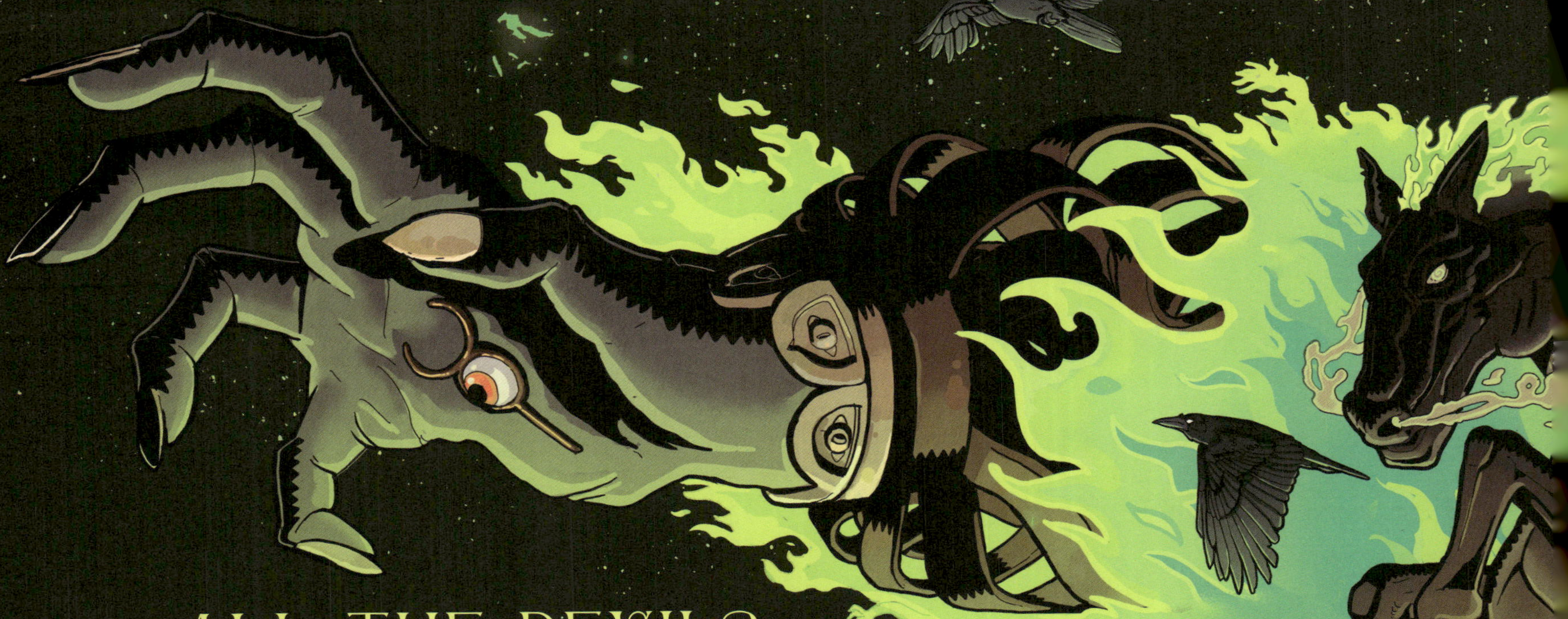

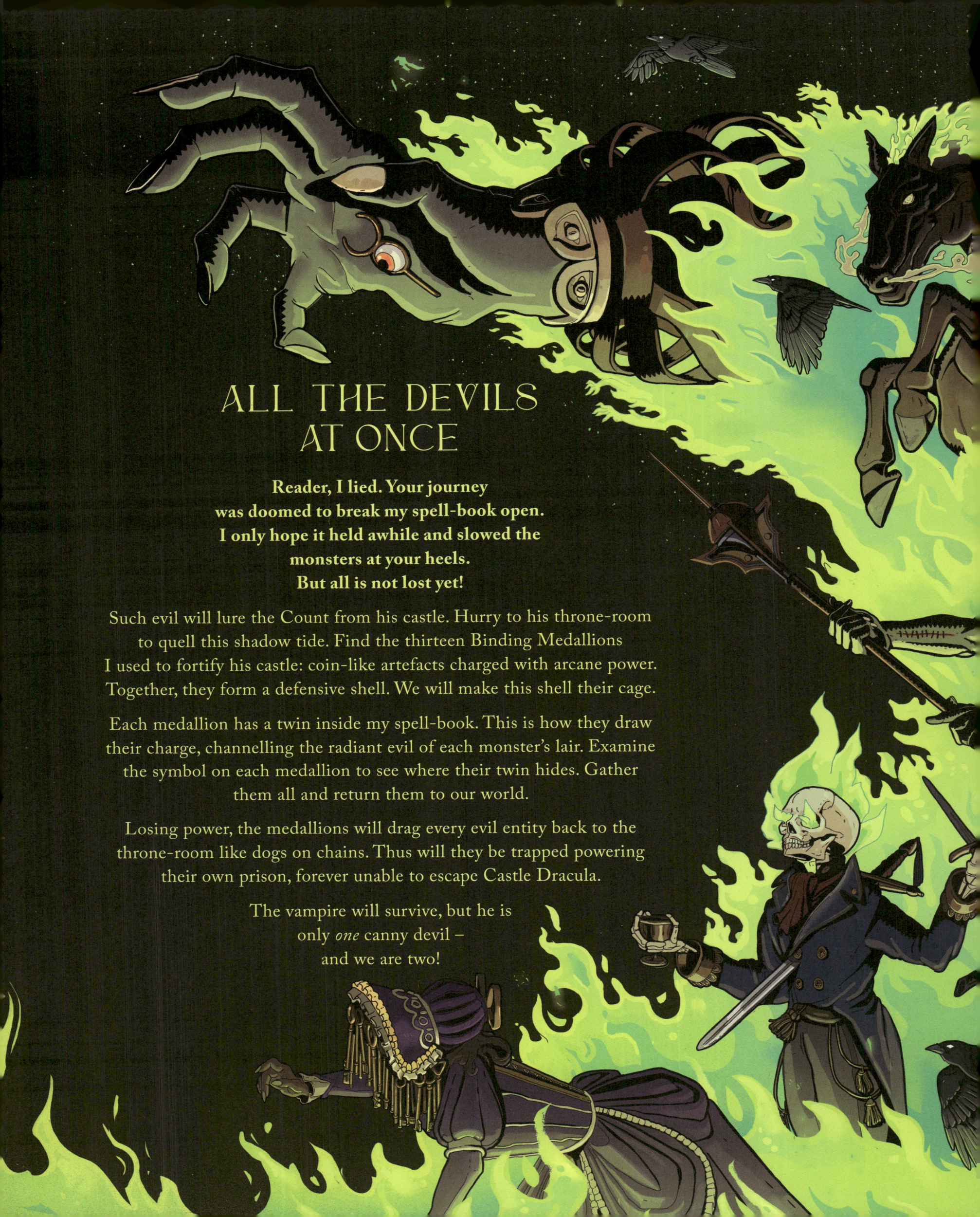

# ALL THE DEVILS AT ONCE

**Reader, I lied. Your journey was doomed to break my spell-book open. I only hope it held awhile and slowed the monsters at your heels. But all is not lost yet!**

Such evil will lure the Count from his castle. Hurry to his throne-room to quell this shadow tide. Find the thirteen Binding Medallions I used to fortify his castle: coin-like artefacts charged with arcane power. Together, they form a defensive shell. We will make this shell their cage.

Each medallion has a twin inside my spell-book. This is how they draw their charge, channelling the radiant evil of each monster's lair. Examine the symbol on each medallion to see where their twin hides. Gather them all and return them to our world.

Losing power, the medallions will drag every evil entity back to the throne-room like dogs on chains. Thus will they be trapped powering their own prison, forever unable to escape Castle Dracula.

The vampire will survive, but he is only *one* canny devil – and we are two!

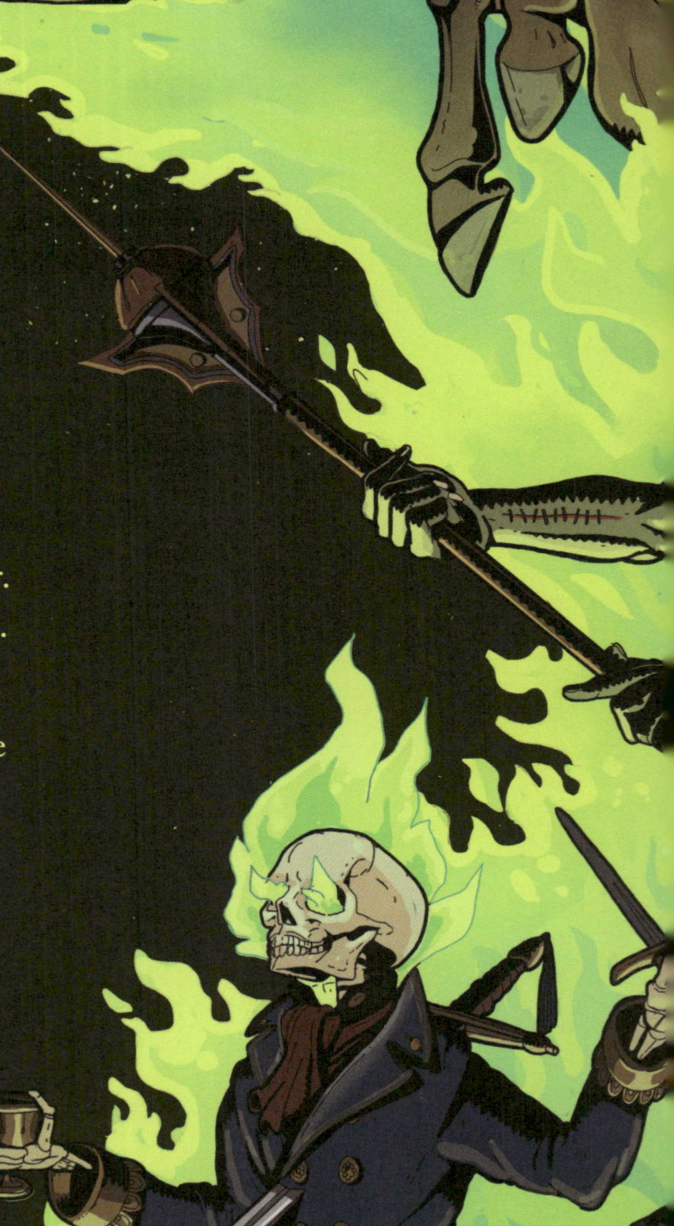

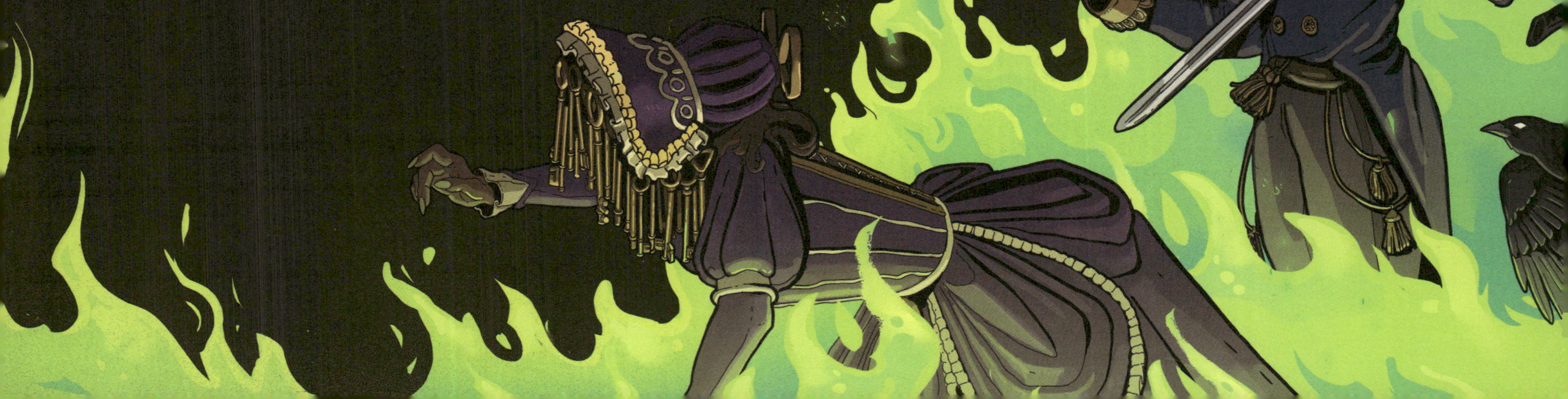

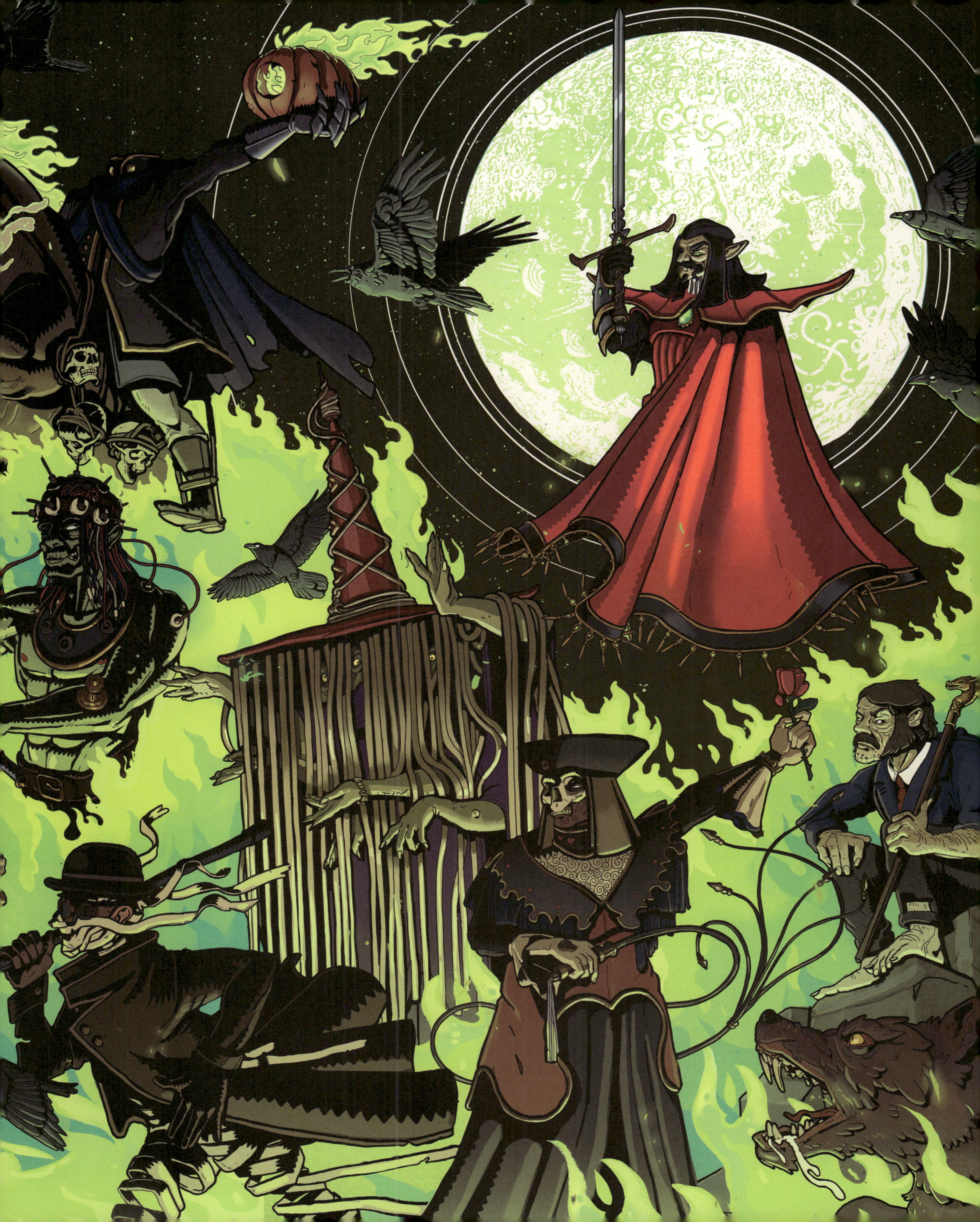

# CASE NOTES

*We learn from failure, not from success!*

'Enter freely and of your own will,' he said...

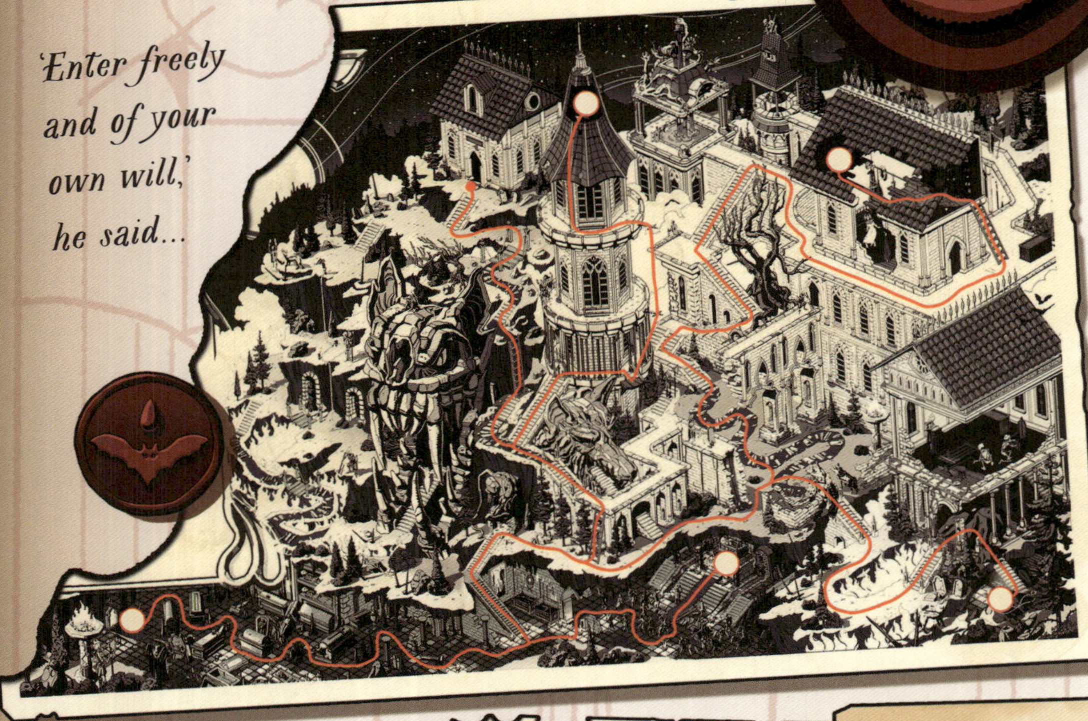

## DR JEKYLL's formula

1: Nitrogen (N)

2: Calcium (Ca)

3: Sulphur (S)

4: Gold (Au)

5: Iron (Fe)

6: Mercury (Hg)

*If he be Mr Hyde, I shall be Mr Seek!*

Once upon a midnight dreary...

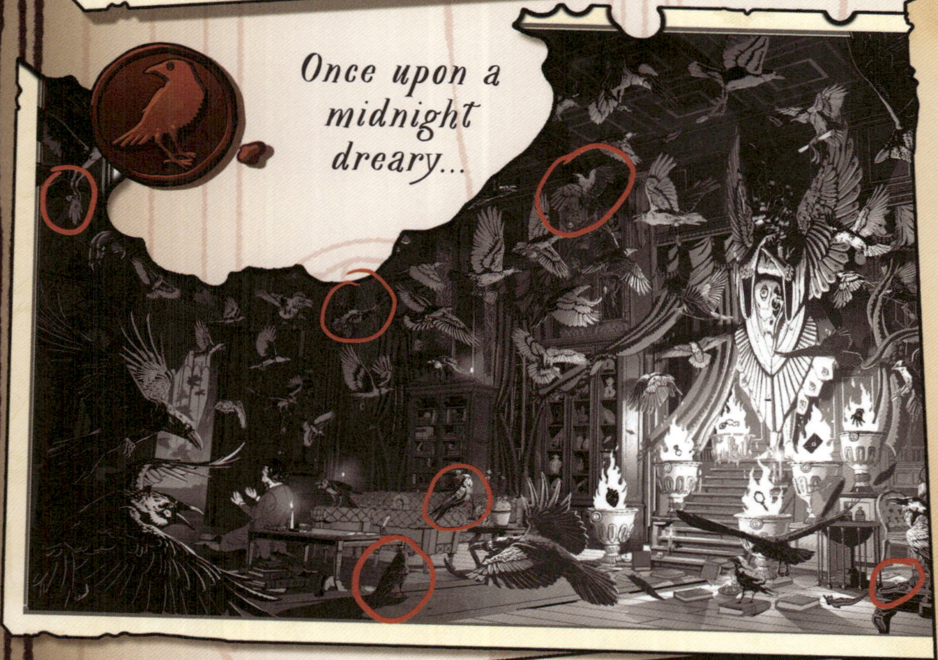

*Not such a hound as mortal eyes have ever seen...*

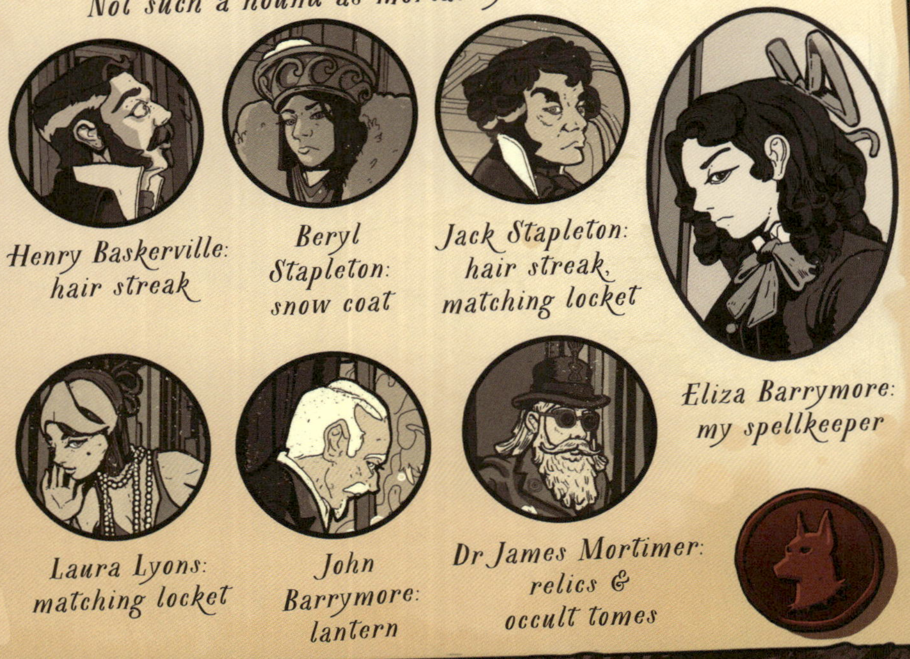

Henry Baskerville: hair streak
Beryl Stapleton: snow coat
Jack Stapleton: hair streak, matching locket
Eliza Barrymore: my spellkeeper
Laura Lyons: matching locket
John Barrymore: lantern
Dr James Mortimer: relics & occult tomes


Vanished in a flash of fire!

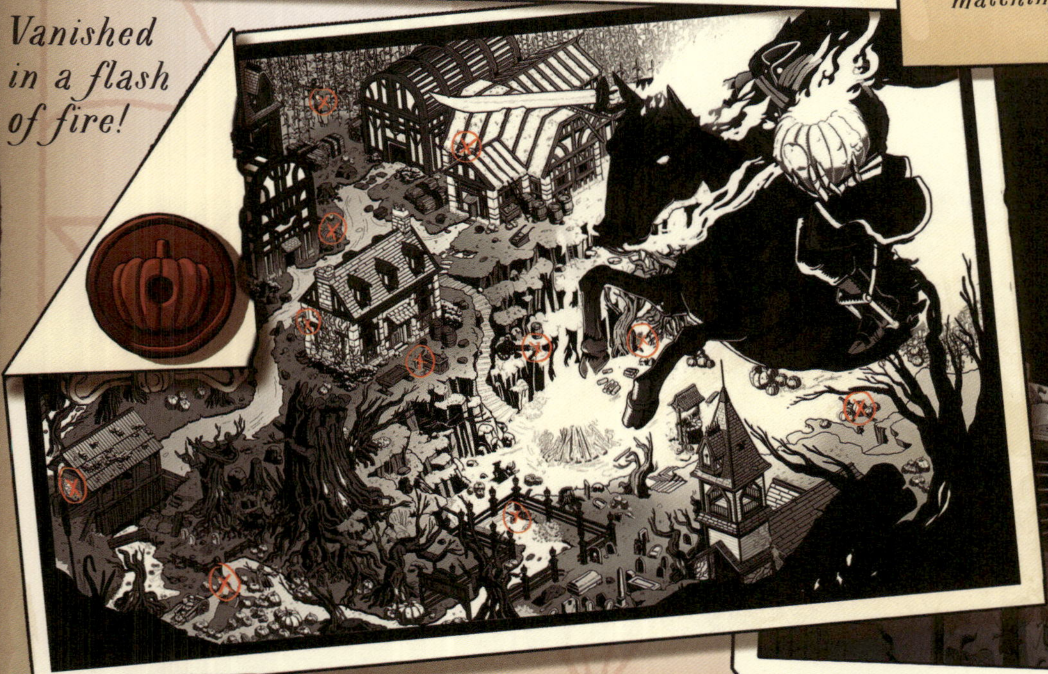

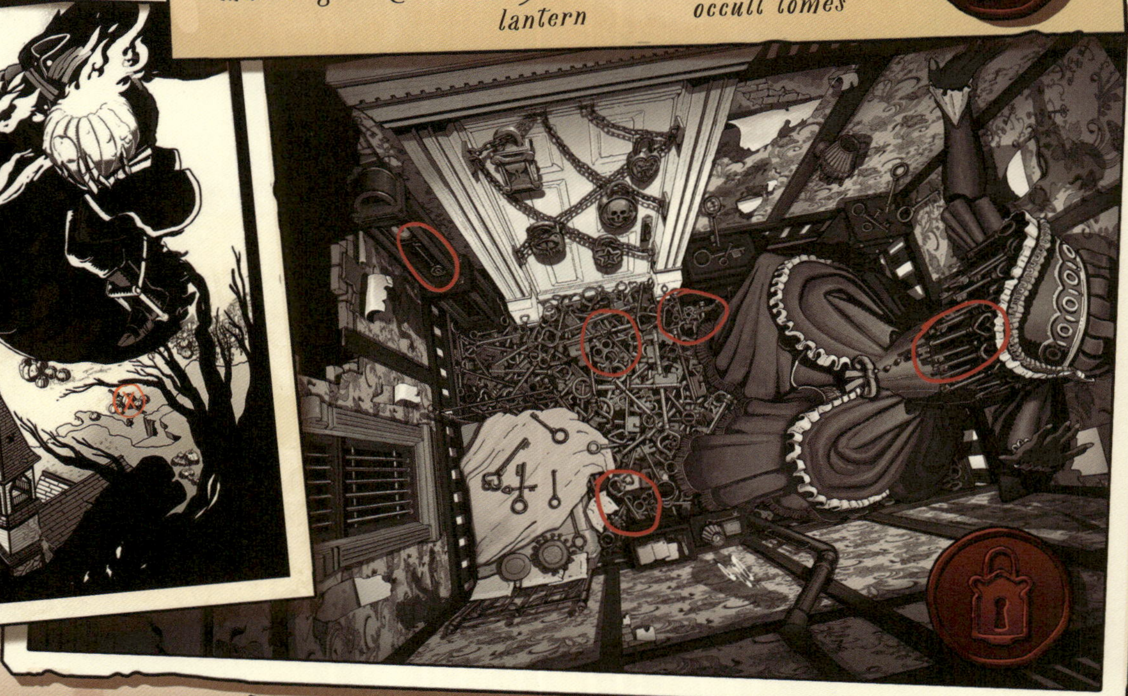

*Those sprawling, flamboyant patterns!*

# MACBETH's fate

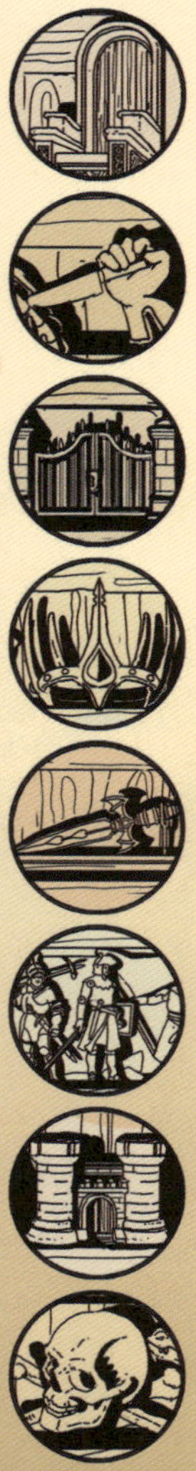

*Throne*

*Murder*

*Gate*

*Crown*

*Dagger*

*Soldiers*

*Castle*

*Death*

*Fair is foul, and foul is fair–*

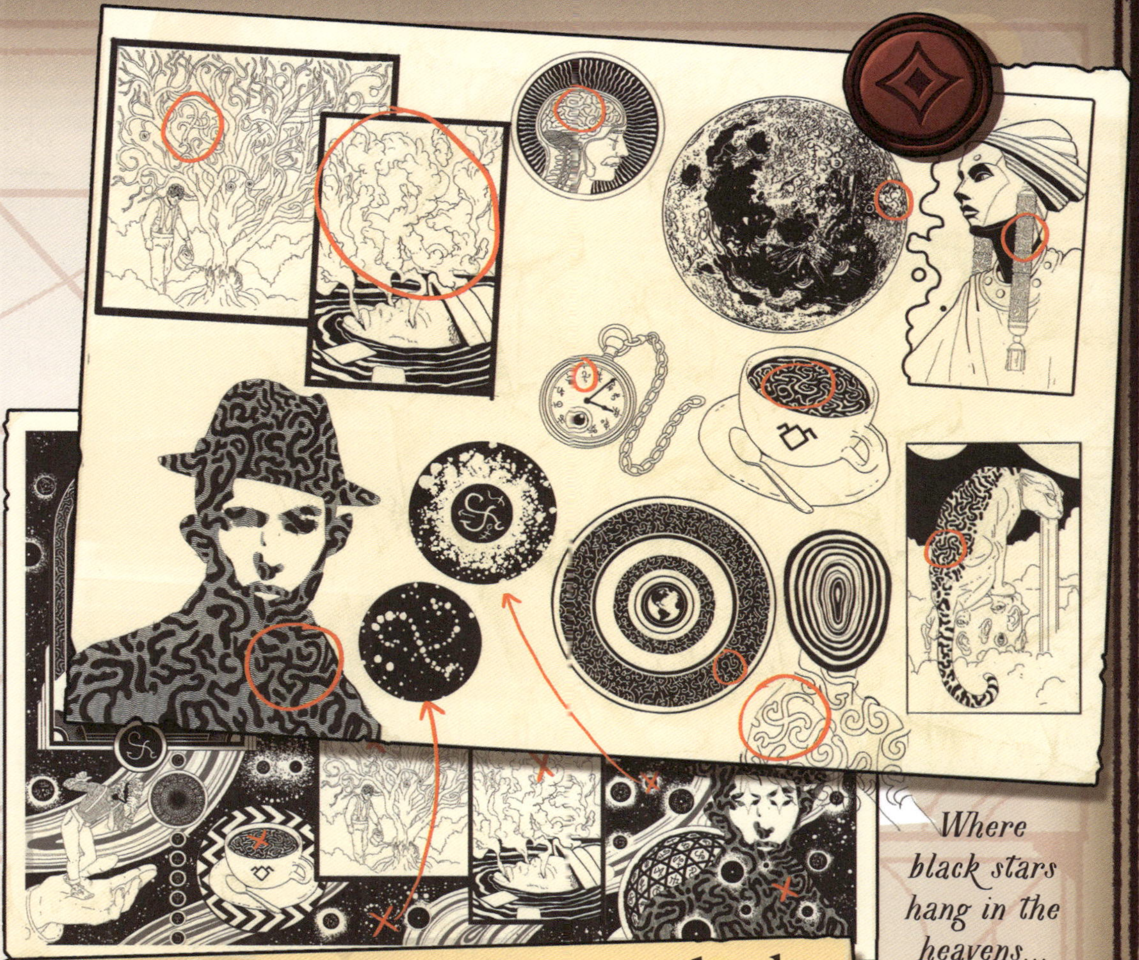

*Where black stars hang in the heavens...*

# THE PHANTOM's melody

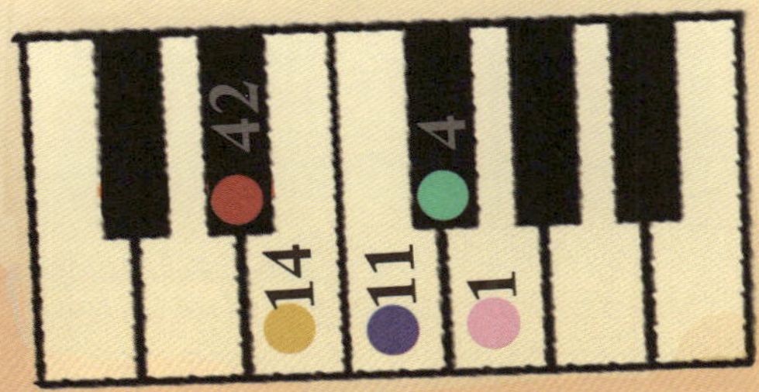

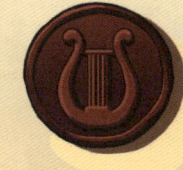

42
4
14
11
1


*A ghost who bleeds is less dangerous!*

*We are unfashioned creatures, but half made up.*

*The mystery, the power, the freedom...*

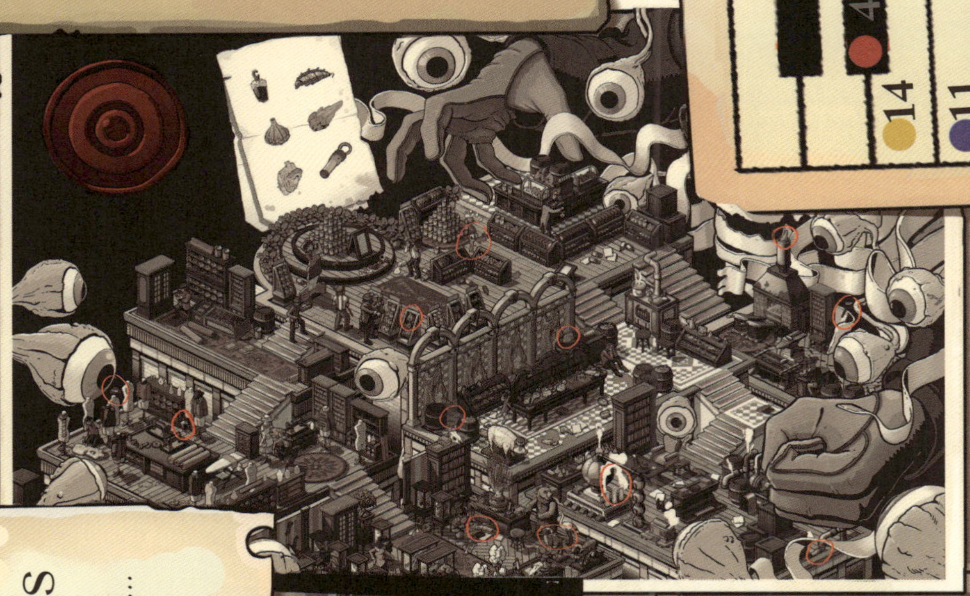

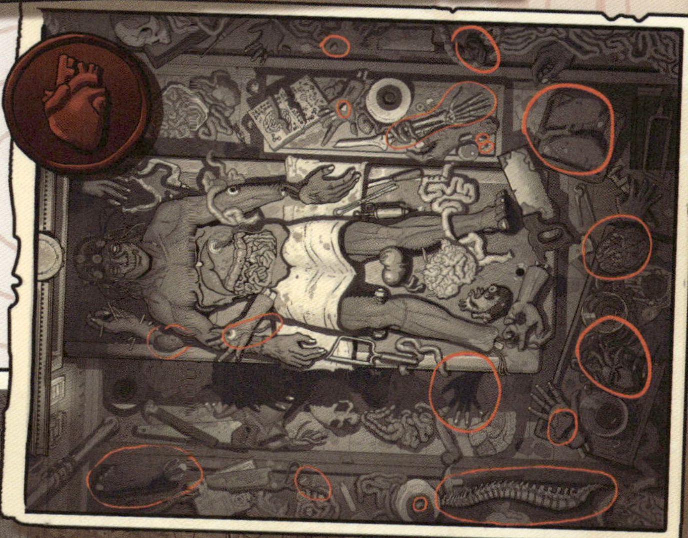

# Dr Johann Faustus

*Hell is just a frame of mind...*

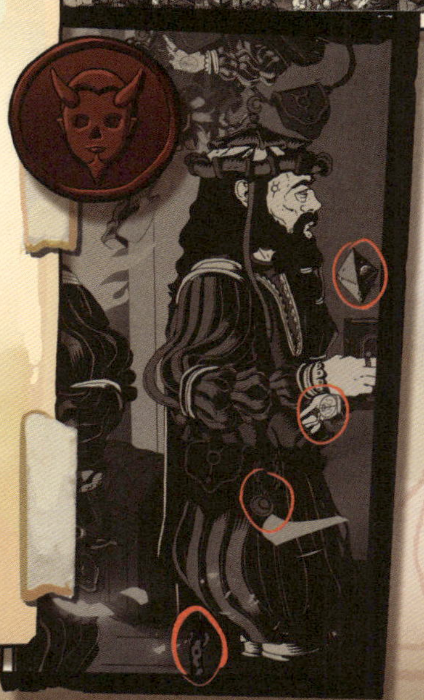

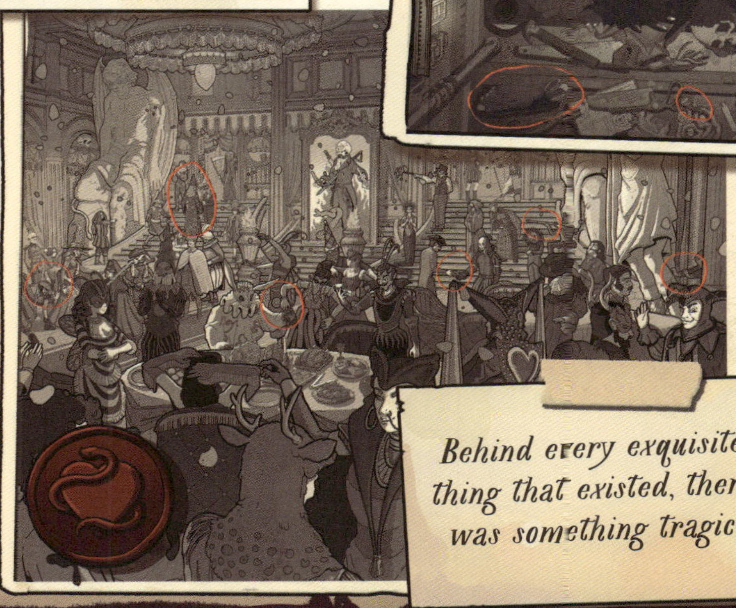

*Behind every exquisite thing that existed, there was something tragic.*

*Note to self: Write back to Captain Nemo of the Nautilus re: treasure under the sea...*